GW01451470

CALLING OF THE ANCIENTS

DEE WHITMAN

CALLING OF THE ANCIENTS

DEW Media

Copyright © 2024 by Dee Whitman

Cover Design by DEW Media as part of SKW Publishing.
All rights reserved. No part of this book may be reproduced in any
manner whatsoever without written permission except in the case
of brief quotations embodied in critical articles and reviews.
First Printing, 2024

CONTENTS

1 – Amman Invite
1

2 – Journey Of Preparation
11

3 – Landing In Amman
21

4 – Meeting The Team
31

5 – Impressions And Clues
39

6 – The Unexpected Discovery
47

7 – Karim's Arrival
55

8 – Danger Danger!
63

9 – A Professor's Insight
73

| v |

10 – Youssef's Warning
83

11 – Close Encounters
91

12 – Deciphering Clues
99

13 – A Family Call
107

14 – Temple Unearthing
115

15 – Ambushed
123

16 – Journeying To The Past
137

17 – Karim Strikes
151

18 – A Professor's Revelation
165

19 – Bonding in the Desert
179

20 – The Treasure Map
193

21 – Through the Canyons
199

22 – Amir's Sacrifice
213

23 – A Hidden Chamber
221

24 – The Final Stand
227

25 – Youssef's Rescue
235

26 – Reclaiming the Artifacts
241

27 – A Farewell with the Doctors
247

28 – Goodbyes and New Beginnings
255

29 – A Family Reunited
263

30 – The Next Chapter
277

Epilogue: Secrets Beneath the Treasury
283

AMMAN INVITE

D r. Ellie Whitcombe was finishing the final chapter of her latest book manuscript when the email arrived. She sat in her small office at the back of their house in Upstate New York, surrounded by stacks of archaeological journals, dusty reference books, and maps with notes scrawled in the margins. It was her haven, a room filled with relics and reminders of past explorations, each item carefully placed and cherished. Simon, her husband, affectionately called it her "treasure cave," a name she thought suited her collection perfectly.

After one last scan of her final paragraph, Ellie leaned back, satisfied. The new book—a blend of history and travel memoir—was her way of sharing stories she and Simon had collected from years of travels. Though fulfilling, the work hadn't completely quenched her thirst for adventure. She missed the mystery and thrill of setting out into unknown landscapes, finding herself surrounded by the whispers of ancient histories waiting to be uncovered.

As if in response to her unspoken wish, a notification chimed. She clicked over to her email and noticed the sender's name: Dr. Nadia al-Masri. Ellie squinted, her mind flipping through memories, trying to recall why the name felt so familiar. Then it clicked—Nadia was a renowned archaeologist she'd met nearly a decade ago at a conference in London. They'd shared an intense but brief conversation, exchanging ideas and dreams about their favorite historical sites, and Nadia had mentioned her ongoing work in the Middle East. Ellie's heart quickened as she opened the message.

Subject: Invitation to Join Archaeological Dig in Amman, Jordan

Dear Dr. Whitcombe,

I hope this message finds you well. My team and I are about to embark on a particularly exciting project here in Amman, and I find myself in need of someone with both historical insight and a genuine passion for archaeology. Your name came to mind, especially given our brief but memorable exchange about shared interests in Near Eastern history.

The project concerns an area of Jordan that has remained largely unexplored. We believe it may hold remnants of a lost temple site, potentially linked to one of the ancient Nabatean cults. It's early yet, but the initial evidence is promising, and we need someone with both analytical and creative insights. In essence, we need a storyteller who can interpret these ancient whispers.

If you're interested, please let me know. I believe this could be a rare, once-in-a-lifetime opportunity to uncover pieces of history that have been hidden for centuries.

Kind regards,

Dr. Nadia al-Masri

Ellie's hands trembled as she finished reading. A surge of excitement washed over her, mixing with memories of long-forgotten dreams. Her thoughts flicked back to a younger version of herself, backpacking through Europe with just a few belongings and a boundless curiosity for ancient ruins, secluded monasteries, and the stories of civilizations long past. That was when she'd met Simon.

In her mind's eye, she could still see him: a quiet young man with a shock of dark, unruly hair and an easy smile, pausing by a crumbling Roman temple in northern Italy, lost in thought as he sketched the ruins in his journal. She'd approached him out of curiosity, intrigued by his patience and focus. They'd exchanged polite conversation, then a few laughs, and before long, they'd realized they were kindred spirits, both fascinated by history and the endless mysteries of the ancient world. Days turned into weeks, and soon, Ellie and Simon found themselves on an unplanned journey together, walking ancient paths, sometimes laughing, sometimes arguing, but always discovering.

Years later, they'd married and raised five children, but Ellie always felt that those early days had set the foundation of who they were—adventurers, seekers of truth, united by a love for each other and for unraveling the past.

Her nostalgia was broken by the sound of footsteps as Simon entered the room, carrying two steaming mugs of coffee. "What's gotten you so captivated?" he asked, placing one of the mugs beside her stack of books.

Ellie turned the screen toward him, her eyes sparkling. "You have to see this."

Simon leaned over her shoulder, his eyebrows lifting as he read the email. When he finished, he turned to her, his gray eyes alight with curiosity. "A dig in Jordan? With Nadia al-Masri? That's not just any invitation, Ellie. She's practically royalty in the world of archaeology."

"Exactly," Ellie replied, a hint of awe in her voice. "She's inviting us—well, me, but I doubt she'd mind if we both went—to join her team in Amman. A temple site, Simon. Imagine the history, the secrets we could uncover!"

Simon chuckled, his fingers tracing the rim of his coffee cup. "And here I thought you were ready to settle down and enjoy being a celebrated author. But I should've known better. Once an explorer, always an explorer."

"You know I'll never lose the itch," Ellie replied, grinning. "And I don't think you've quite let go of it, either."

He gave a small shrug, but she could see the familiar gleam of excitement in his eyes. Simon had always been the grounded one, the steady rock to her endless curiosity, yet he too had a restless spirit. In their twenties, they'd made time for little adventures even after marriage and children—hiking trails, exploring ruins, discovering local histories. Though their life was rich with family, a part of them both still craved the thrill of discovery.

"Well," Simon said, "are you going to accept?"

Ellie hesitated, her thoughts flickering to their family, their responsibilities, and the cozy, predictable life they'd grown accustomed to. Then she laughed, shaking her head. "What am I even hesitating for? Of course, I'm accepting!"

Later that evening, they set up FaceTime calls with their children, beginning with their eldest, Oliver, who appeared on the screen with a skeptical frown.

"Mom, Dad, isn't Jordan...dangerous?" Oliver asked, glancing at them with the protective tone he'd taken on since he was a boy.

"Oliver, Jordan is perfectly safe," Ellie reassured him. "It's an official dig, and we'll be with experts the entire time. Besides, they're not sending us out into the desert alone."

He sighed, though a small smile broke through his concern. "Alright, just promise me you'll stay in touch. I want regular updates."

Sophie, their second-born, called next, with her toddler, Jacob, perched on her lap. "Promise you'll stay safe, okay?" she asked, the worry in her voice unmistakable. "Jacob and I need his adventurous grandparents to come back in one piece!"

They laughed, promising to take care, and continued with the rest of their calls. Benjamin, Isabel, and Nathan were all enthusiastic, each encouraging them with pride and excitement. Their youngest, Nathan, simply grinned and said, "Finally, someone's out there living our family dream. Bring me back a piece of the past, will you?"

With her heart racing, Ellie typed out her response to Dr. al-Masri:

Dear Dr. al-Masri,

Thank you so much for the invitation. My husband Simon and I would be honored to join your team in Amman. We both share a deep fascination with the ancient Near East, and the opportunity to participate in such a meaningful dig is truly a privilege.

We'll begin making travel arrangements as soon as possible and look forward to discussing the details with you.

Warm regards,

Dr. Ellie Whitcombe

When she pressed "Send," Ellie felt a rush of excitement. The call to adventure had sounded, and they had answered.

They couldn't contain their enthusiasm. Rather than winding down for the evening, Ellie and Simon found themselves diving into a research frenzy, eager to familiarize themselves with Nadia's work and the rich history of Jordan. They sat side by side, huddled over her laptop, as articles, photographs, and journal entries from Nadia's past digs filled the screen.

"Look at this one," Simon said, pointing to a photo from a past excavation led by Nadia. It showed a carved Nabatean artifact covered in intricate symbols that seemed to leap off the stone. "This was from her excavation near Petra a few years back. She theorized these inscriptions were part of a forgotten language, possibly a dialect used only in ceremonial contexts."

Ellie leaned in, captivated. "That's incredible. If she's inviting us to join a dig she considers equally significant, we might be about to uncover some unknown aspect of Nabatean culture."

Simon's eyes gleamed. "This could be bigger than anything we've been part of before."

Excitement bubbled between them, and Ellie couldn't help but recall the sense of wonder she'd felt during their earliest days together, roaming through Europe's ruins. Even now, decades later, the spark of discovery felt just as exhilarating.

After an hour of scouring articles and digging up more about Nadia's accomplishments, Simon pulled up an episode of Expedition Unknown featuring Josh Gates investigating lost cities in the Middle East. "This is the episode where he looks for the tomb of Alexander the Great in Egypt," Simon said, pressing play. "It's not Jordan, but it's close enough to get us in the mindset."

They settled in, watching as Josh Gates navigated the desert, interviewing locals, and following ancient legends. The more they watched, the more the Whitcombes found themselves leaning forward, as though sharing in the thrill of exploration. Every new lead, every piece of evidence, felt like a glimpse into their own upcoming journey.

Just as the episode wrapped, Ellie nudged Simon. "There's another one—let's see if we can find any of Bettany Hughes's episodes on Jordan."

Bettany Hughes, a respected historian and archaeologist, was well-known for her documentaries on ancient civilizations. Ellie found one of Hughes's episodes that explored Jordan, covering the history and culture of the Nabateans, and they clicked on it eagerly. The opening scenes showed Hughes walking through Petra, her voice describing the ancient marvels as though weaving a story from another time.

"Look at that," Ellie murmured, watching as Hughes traced her fingers over Nabatean inscriptions on the stone. "She makes everything feel so alive, like she's drawing the past into the present."

As Hughes continued her journey, passing Petra's rock-cut tombs and winding paths, Simon and Ellie absorbed every word, every visual detail. Hughes spoke of the Nabateans' skills as traders, architects, and guardians of hidden knowledge—a civilization that had left behind breathtaking works yet remained shrouded in mystery.

Simon turned to Ellie with an animated smile. "Can you believe this is actually happening? In just a few days, we'll be doing the same thing—hunting for clues, uncovering history."

Ellie grinned, unable to contain her excitement. "And with Nadia al-Masri, no less! It feels like a dream. Imagine if we find a site that links to something as extraordinary as Petra—only untouched, as if waiting for us specifically."

They watched a second Bettany Hughes episode, one covering sites near Amman itself. The city's vibrant history came alive through Hughes's descriptions of its ancient temples and the ruins surrounding it, hinting at a blend of cultures and influences. The scenes filled them with awe, sparking fresh ideas about what their own adventure could hold.

Simon paused the video during a segment about hidden artifacts, turning to Ellie with a pensive look. "We've read so much about Jordanian history, but something about watching it here feels real, doesn't it? We'll be right in the thick of it. Do you think we're prepared?"

Ellie nodded, squeezing his hand. "More than prepared. We've been to digs before, but something about this feels different, almost... fated." Her voice softened as she continued. "The fact that Nadia reached out to us, after all these years—it's like everything we've done has led to this moment."

Simon's expression mirrored her own sense of awe. "Then let's embrace it. This could be our most significant adventure yet."

They fell into an animated discussion about what they might find, each idea grander than the last. In their minds, they explored hidden temples, unearthed forgotten relics, and uncovered stories that had long been buried in the sands. And as they spoke, the dream of their upcoming journey took on a life of its own, as vivid as any expedition they'd embarked on in the past.

It was well past midnight by the time they finally closed the laptop, their minds still racing with excitement. The thrill of discovery hung in the air, and as they shared a smile, they knew they were ready for whatever lay ahead.

2

JOURNEY OF
PREPARATION

Ellie sat at the kitchen table, sipping her coffee as she mentally mapped out the conversations that lay ahead. She and Simon would have to share the news with their five children, each of whom, she was sure, would have their own distinct reaction. The more she thought about it, the more she realized how revealing this conversation might be about each child's character, personality, and unique relationship with their parents.

Simon entered the kitchen, carrying a notepad where he'd listed time zones and optimal moments to contact each of their kids. "Alright," he said with a grin, "I think

I've cracked the code of time zones and schedules. Oliver should be free now, if we're ready to start?"

Ellie nodded, glancing at her phone. "Let's do it. Might as well start with our resident skeptic."

With a deep breath, Ellie hit the button to call their eldest, Oliver, who picked up almost immediately. His face appeared on the screen, sporting a slightly exasperated expression that was all too familiar. Despite the lines of responsibility etched into his features, his dark hair and serious demeanor reminded her so much of Simon in his younger days.

"Mom, Dad, what's up?" he asked, not one for pleasantries. He glanced at the clock in the background. "Calling me early on a Saturday—this must be big."

Ellie smiled. "It is. We wanted to share some news with you." She paused, feeling a slight rush of excitement mixed with anticipation. "Your dad and I have been invited to join an archaeological dig in Jordan."

Oliver blinked, clearly taken aback. "Wait—Jordan? As in the Middle East?"

Simon chuckled. "Yes, the Middle East. It's a dig with a renowned archaeologist, Dr. Nadia al-Masri. You remember we mentioned her a while back?"

Oliver's brows furrowed as he absorbed this. "I know who she is. But... are you sure this is safe? I mean, you two haven't exactly been on a big expedition in years."

Ellie felt a pang, but she chose to take his words in stride. "Oliver, we'll be fine. Jordan is a stable country, and we'll be with a professional team the entire time. We'll have secure accommodations, and they're setting everything up with experts."

Oliver's expression softened, though his worry remained. "I just... want you to be careful. I know you two are adventurers at heart, but you're not exactly in your twenties anymore."

Simon laughed, shaking his head. "We may be a bit older, but we've still got a lot of spirit left, Ollie."

Reluctantly, Oliver smiled. "Alright. But promise me you'll keep in touch. I want updates, especially if anything unexpected happens."

Ellie and Simon nodded, sharing a look of understanding. "Of course," Ellie said. "We'll keep you in the loop. And maybe you'll even see a side of the world you've only read about through our eyes."

The call ended on a promising note, though Ellie knew Oliver would worry. He always had a strong sense of responsibility, a trait she admired yet one that often added weight to his shoulders.

Next was Sophie, their second-born, a gentle soul with a caring nature and a fierce protectiveness over her family. Her face appeared on the screen, her toddler, Jacob, perched on her lap. The little boy looked up at the screen, waving enthusiastically.

"Hi, Mom! Hi, Dad!" Sophie's smile was warm, though it quickly faded when she noticed her parents' expressions. "What's going on? You both look... excited. What are you up to?"

Ellie grinned, catching Simon's eye. "You caught us. We have some exciting news."

"Mom and Dad are going on an adventure!" Simon announced playfully.

Sophie's eyes widened, immediately switching to "mom" mode as she leaned closer to the screen. "Adventure? Where? What do you mean?"

Ellie chuckled. "We've been invited to join an archaeological dig in Amman, Jordan. It's with Dr. Nadia al-Masri—"

"Wait, Jordan?" Sophie interrupted, her voice filled with concern. "That's... Isn't that dangerous? Are you sure this is a good idea?"

"Sophie," Ellie replied gently, "Jordan is safe. It's one of the more stable countries in the Middle East, and we'll be with a team of professionals the whole time. We'll be perfectly fine."

Sophie's brows knit together as she glanced down at Jacob, who was babbling happily, unaware of the conversation's weight. "I know you'll be with a team, but... I just worry about you. It's so far away. And archaeology—there's so much that could go wrong."

Ellie could see the fear in Sophie's eyes, and she softened her tone. "Sophie, we appreciate your concern. I promise you, we'll be careful. This isn't some reckless expedition. Dr. al-Masri is an expert, and she's arranging everything with safety in mind."

Sophie nodded slowly, though the worry hadn't left her face. "I know you're both adventurous. I just want you to come back safely."

"Promise you'll keep in touch?" she added, her voice small.

"Promise," Simon said, his voice full of warmth. "We'll be back in one piece, with stories to tell Jacob when he's older."

Sophie smiled, though a hint of worry remained. Ellie knew Sophie's anxiety was rooted in love, and it filled her with gratitude for the bond they shared.

Next, they called Benjamin, their middle child, who had always been a free spirit with a natural curiosity about the world. Benjamin picked up the call while sitting in a cluttered room, surrounded by books, a guitar, and what looked like half-assembled sculptures.

"Mom! Dad!" he greeted, looking genuinely thrilled. "What's the news? You both look like you've got something brewing."

Simon grinned. "How do you feel about your parents joining an archaeological dig?"

Benjamin's eyes lit up. "No way! That's awesome. Where?"

"Amman, Jordan," Ellie replied, smiling at his excitement.

"Jordan!" Benjamin whistled, shaking his head. "That's incredible. I'm actually jealous. Imagine all the ancient relics, the hidden histories waiting to be unearthed."

Ellie chuckled, her heart warmed by his enthusiasm. "I thought you'd be the most excited about this. Dr. Nadia al-Masri invited us, and we couldn't say no."

Benjamin nodded, visibly impressed. "You couldn't have asked for a better opportunity. You two are living the dream, honestly."

Ellie's smile grew. "Thanks, Ben. We're thrilled too. It feels like a once-in-a-lifetime adventure."

"Promise you'll document everything," Benjamin said eagerly. "Pictures, notes, drawings. And bring back something cool, alright?"

"We'll do our best," Simon said with a laugh. "And you'll be the first to see whatever we bring back."

Their conversation with Benjamin left Ellie feeling buoyed by his boundless enthusiasm. Of all their children, Benjamin understood their love for exploration most naturally. His own life was an adventure, full of creativity and curiosity—a spirit she and Simon had always encouraged.

Their second-to-last call was with Isabel, who had chosen a career in environmental science and was dedicated to protecting the earth's resources. Her practicality and a deep-seated sense of purpose often made her the voice of reason among her siblings.

"Hi, Mom. Hi, Dad," Isabel said, her face appearing on the screen. She was dressed in her usual simple, earthy tones, with her hair pulled back in a practical ponytail.

"Hi, sweetie," Ellie began, smiling. "We have some news for you."

Isabel tilted her head, listening intently. "Oh? What's going on?"

Ellie took a breath, then shared the news of their upcoming journey to Jordan, watching Isabel's face for her reaction.

"Wow," Isabel said, a genuine look of surprise crossing her features. "That's... I didn't expect you two to go on a big expedition again."

"Neither did we," Simon admitted. "But the opportunity came up, and it just felt right."

Isabel nodded thoughtfully. "I think it sounds amazing. But you're both going to be careful, right? The climate in that region can be harsh, and I'm sure the conditions are physically demanding."

Ellie smiled, touched by her concern. "We're fully prepared. We're packing all the essentials—hydration packs, durable clothing, first aid kits. We'll be ready."

Isabel's practical nature wouldn't let her accept that answer without further reassurance. "Good. Just make sure you're both mindful of the heat and take all the safety precautions. I'd hate for you to get sick or dehydrated."

"Don't worry," Simon replied, smiling. "We'll have all the necessary protections, and we'll check in regularly."

Isabel gave a rare grin. "Alright. I'm actually proud of you both. You're seizing an adventure that most people would only dream of."

Their conversation ended on a high note, with Isabel wishing them safe travels and reminding them to stay environmentally conscious during their dig—a reminder that brought a shared chuckle.

Finally, they called Nathan, their youngest and perhaps the most unabashedly optimistic of the family. When he picked up, his broad smile was already in place.

"Mom! Dad! What's up?" Nathan greeted, leaning close to the camera, his energy practically radiating through the screen.

Ellie smiled back, feeling her heart swell with affection for her "baby." "We've got an exciting adventure to share with you. How does an archaeological dig in Jordan sound?"

Nathan's face lit up, his grin widening. "Jordan? You're kidding! That's incredible! So you two are going to be exploring temples and digging up ancient stuff?"

Ellie laughed, nodding. "Yes, exactly. We'll be working with Dr. Nadia al-Masri, who's invited us to help uncover an ancient temple site. We'll be searching for relics and possibly discovering new pieces of history."

Nathan let out a delighted whoop. "That's amazing! You guys are going to be like Indiana Jones or something. Promise you'll tell me everything, okay?"

Simon chuckled. "Of course, Nathan. You'll be our first call when we make any big discoveries."

Their youngest son's enthusiasm was infectious, filling them with renewed excitement for the journey ahead. "You're both inspiring, you know that?" Nathan said, his face softening. "I'm proud of you two for following your hearts."

"Thanks, honey," Ellie replied, her voice thick with emotion. "We're proud of you too."

When the call ended, Ellie and Simon sat together in a comfortable silence, reflecting on the conversations with their children. Each response had been a reminder of the unique qualities that defined their family: Oliver's protectiveness, Sophie's deep concern, Benjamin's creative energy, Isabel's practicality, and Nathan's unflagging optimism. In every reaction, Ellie felt the love and support of her family, even if mixed with worry and questions.

"Looks like we have a lot of supporters," Simon said, wrapping his arm around Ellie's shoulder.

Ellie nodded, feeling her heart swell. "We're incredibly lucky."

They shared a quiet smile, comforted by the thought that, no matter what awaited them in Jordan, they had the encouragement and love of their family, standing behind them like a solid foundation.

LANDING IN AMMAN

The morning of their departure dawned clear and bright, casting warm light through the windows of their cozy home in Upstate New York. Ellie and Simon exchanged a look as they closed the door behind them, the click of the lock carrying a finality that made their hearts race with anticipation. The driveway was lined with fall leaves, and Ellie took in one last glance, smiling to herself. This journey felt different—a leap into a mystery, with each step taking them further from the familiar.

The airport was a whirlwind of excitement as they navigated security and checked in their luggage, their minds spinning with thoughts of what lay ahead. Boarding their flight, they shared a grin, both sensing that this trip would become one of their most treasured memories. The plane taxied down the runway, and soon they felt the rush of acceleration as it lifted into the air, the world below shrinking beneath them.

At cruising altitude, a flight attendant approached with a knowing smile, offering them glasses of champagne. "To toast the journey, perhaps?" she suggested, setting down the flutes with a sparkle in her eye.

Ellie raised her glass toward Simon. "To adventure and the thrill of the unknown," she said, her voice brimming with excitement.

Simon clinked his glass with hers. "To Jordan, to unearthing the past, and to whatever secrets await us," he replied with a grin, his eyes full of anticipation.

They sipped their champagne, and for a moment, the buzz of the plane faded as they sank into a comfortable silence, each lost in thoughts of what they hoped to discover. The reality of their departure, their commitment to uncovering something beyond their understanding, settled in fully, making each mile seem like a step closer to an era long gone.

Hours passed as they journeyed across continents, and somewhere over the Atlantic, Ellie pulled out her notebook, jotting down ideas and sketching symbols she imagined might await them at the dig site. Simon leaned over, peering at her sketches with curiosity.

"Think we'll find anything close to that?" he asked, raising an eyebrow at her detailed drawings of ancient symbols she'd imagined in the moments before falling asleep.

Ellie laughed, shaking her head. "Who knows? Maybe even something grander. After all, Nadia's invitation hinted at something tied to an ancient temple, and who knows what the Nabateans left behind?"

The hours passed with snatches of sleep, conversations about the dig, and dreams of their upcoming adventure. Each time Ellie woke and glanced out the window, the scenery below had shifted, an ever-changing tapestry as they edged closer to Jordan.

At last, the plane began its descent, and a voice came over the intercom announcing their approach into Amman. Ellie pressed her face to the window, her eyes widening as the city came into view—a tapestry of sandy beige and golden hues, buildings nestled together like pieces of an intricate mosaic stretching far into the distance.

Beside her, Simon was equally captivated, leaning forward to get a better view. "Look at that," he murmured, his voice filled with quiet awe. "It's like something from a dream."

Ellie smiled, sharing his sentiment. After hours in the air, they'd finally arrived, and the sight of Amman felt like a doorway opening into another world. This was it—the adventure they'd both longed for. And now that they were here, a sense of anticipation hung between them, thick and buzzing.

As they disembarked, the warm, dry air enveloped them like a gentle embrace, carrying with it the faint scent of spices, dust, and something earthy and ancient. Ellie took a deep breath, savoring the mix of smells, feeling herself fully anchored in the present. She was here, in Jordan, ready to dive into a world of buried secrets and undiscovered history.

"Excited?" Simon asked, a knowing smile tugging at his lips.

"More than you can imagine," Ellie replied, her eyes sparkling.

They navigated through customs and retrieved their bags, marveling at how the airport bustled with a blend of travelers from every corner of the globe—backpackers with dusty boots, families greeting each other with hugs, and locals moving with practiced ease through the crowds. The variety of languages, outfits, and cultures reminded them of how vast and varied the world truly was.

Once they reached the exit, Ellie's gaze landed on a man holding a modest sign that read "Whitcombe." He was older, perhaps in his sixties, with dark hair peppered with gray and a warm smile that immediately put them at ease. Dressed in a neatly pressed button-down shirt and slacks, he seemed to radiate kindness.

"Dr. Ellie and Dr. Simon Whitcombe?" he asked as they approached, his voice carrying a warm, slightly accented tone.

"That's us," Simon replied, extending his hand. "And you must be Youssef?"

The man nodded, taking Simon's hand in a firm, friendly shake. "Indeed. Welcome to Amman! It's a pleasure to meet you both." He turned to Ellie, offering her a respectful nod. "You are here for the dig, yes? I'm told it will be something extraordinary."

Ellie smiled, feeling an immediate connection to him. "Yes, and we're grateful to have you with us, Youssef. We've heard so much about Jordan's beauty."

He laughed, his eyes crinkling with warmth. "Oh, you are in for a treat, then. Amman is beautiful, but it's only the beginning. Jordan has many secrets, each with a story to tell. And I am more than happy to help you find them."

Youssef led them to his taxi, a well-kept sedan with a few Arabic charms hanging from the rearview mirror. As they settled into the back seat, Ellie took in the small details—the worn leather seats, the subtle scent of cardamom from a coffee cup in the console, the faint strains of Arabic music playing softly through the speakers. Each piece added to the mosaic of Jordanian life that was unfolding around her.

The car pulled out into the flow of traffic, and Ellie's eyes were immediately drawn to the world outside the window. Amman's streets were a bustling blend of old and new. Ancient stone buildings stood proudly beside sleek modern shops, their facades bathed in the golden glow of the rising sun. Narrow streets twisted and wound up hillsides, lined with stalls selling everything from fresh produce to intricately woven carpets. Vendors called out to passersby, and children wove through the crowd, their laughter echoing through the air.

"Amman is a city of contrasts," Youssef explained as he navigated the winding roads. "You will see many layers here. The ancient and the modern. The quiet streets and the bustling markets. It's a city with a spirit, one that welcomes you with open arms."

Ellie nodded, entranced by his words. She could feel the city's pulse, its heartbeat thrumming beneath the surface. Amman was alive in a way she hadn't experienced before—its history interwoven with its present, its people carrying forward the legacy of those who'd come before them.

As they drove deeper into the city, Youssef pointed out various landmarks, sharing stories that hinted at the depth of Amman's history. "There, you see that hill? It is called Jabal Amman. One of the oldest areas of the city. And over there is the Amman Citadel—one of our most treasured sites. It has seen thousands of years, from the time of the Romans to the present day."

Ellie's gaze followed his pointing finger, and her heart raced as she caught sight of the Citadel—a cluster of ancient ruins perched on a hill, bathed in the soft light of the morning sun. She could see columns stretching up toward the sky, remnants of a temple that had once stood as a monument to gods long forgotten.

"Will we have time to explore?" she asked, her excitement barely contained.

Youssef chuckled. "You will have plenty of time. Jordan is full of places like this. The Citadel, Petra, Wadi Rum... Each one has its own spirit, its own story. But," he added with a sly smile, "the real secrets are often hidden from view. Only those who seek them with an open heart can find them."

Ellie exchanged a glance with Simon, who was equally captivated. "Then we're definitely in the right place," she said, smiling.

They soon arrived at their guesthouse, a small but charming building nestled in one of Amman's quieter neighborhoods. The guesthouse owner, a woman named Amina, greeted them warmly, her hospitality evident as she helped them settle into their room. The room was simple yet cozy, with crisp linens, a woven rug, and a large window that opened onto a view of the city's hillsides.

Once they'd unpacked, they stepped outside to explore, taking Youssef's recommendation to stroll through the local souk, or market, just a short walk away. Ellie's senses came alive the moment they entered. The scent of spices wafted through the air, mingling with the aroma of freshly baked bread and grilled meats. Vendors called out in a blend of Arabic and English, their voices creating a rhythmic melody that hummed above the steady flow of footsteps and laughter.

They wandered between stalls, captivated by the sheer variety of goods on display. Piles of saffron and cumin were stacked like small mountains beside baskets of dried figs, dates, and apricots. Colorful fabrics fluttered in the breeze, each one a masterpiece of intricate patterns and vibrant hues.

Ellie's fingers brushed over the textures as they walked, her mind racing with wonder. It was as if each item carried a story of its own—of hands that had woven, crafted, and cultivated these treasures from the land itself. She paused at a small stall selling jewelry, her eyes drawn to a silver pendant etched with ancient symbols.

"Interested?" the vendor asked, his eyes twinkling.

Ellie picked up the pendant, admiring the detailed craftsmanship. "It's beautiful. Do these symbols mean anything?"

The vendor nodded, his expression thoughtful. "Yes, they are symbols of protection. Passed down from our ancestors. They believed these signs would guard the wearer from harm, protect them on their journey."

Ellie smiled, charmed by the notion. She purchased the pendant, slipping it around her neck, feeling its cool weight against her skin. It felt like a small piece of Amman's spirit, a token to carry with her as she and Simon began this new chapter of their lives.

As they continued to explore, they came upon a small café tucked away on a quiet side street. Simon suggested they stop for tea, and they settled into a cozy corner, watching the ebb and flow of life pass by through the open window. The waiter brought them glasses of tea flavored with mint and cardamom, the fragrant steam rising in delicate curls.

"Cheers to new beginnings," Simon said, raising his glass.

Ellie clinked her glass with his, her heart swelling with gratitude. "To new beginnings," she echoed, feeling the warmth of the tea spread through her, grounding her in this moment.

They spent the afternoon exploring, taking in the sights and sounds of Amman, marveling at the layers of history embedded in its streets. Everywhere they turned, they were met with remnants of the past—ancient ruins nestled between modern buildings, alleyways that seemed to hold whispers of stories long forgotten.

As the sun began to dip below the horizon, casting a warm, golden glow over the city, they returned to the guesthouse, tired but exhilarated. Their first day in Jordan had been everything they'd hoped for and more, a rich tapestry of colors, scents, and sounds that filled them with a sense of wonder.

Just before they retired for the night, Ellie took a moment to step out onto their small balcony, taking in the view of Amman's hillsides bathed in the soft glow of dusk. She closed her eyes, breathing in the night air, feeling a quiet peace settle over her.

This was where they were meant to be—on the brink of a discovery, standing at the threshold of a new adventure, with the promise of ancient secrets waiting to be uncovered.

Back inside, Simon joined her, his arm slipping around her shoulders. They stood together, sharing a comfortable silence, each lost in their own thoughts.

"We're really here," Ellie whispered, her voice filled with awe.

Simon nodded, his voice gentle. "Yes. And something tells me we're about to uncover more than just artifacts."

Ellie leaned into him, feeling the truth in his words. This wasn't just about history or discovery—it was about following a calling, a pull that had led them halfway across the world. Together, they were stepping into the unknown, hand in hand, with open hearts and open minds.

As they turned in for the night, they felt a deep sense of peace and purpose. Amman had welcomed them warmly, and they were ready—ready to uncover the stories buried in the sand, to connect with the lives that had walked these paths before them, and to see where this journey would take them.

MEETING THE TEAM

The next morning, Ellie and Simon awoke to a warm breeze wafting through their window, carrying with it the faint scent of spices and a hint of the desert. They felt a quiet excitement brewing, the kind that came with the anticipation of stepping into a world they'd only dreamed of. Today, they would meet Dr. Nadia al-Masri and her team, and Ellie felt a flutter of nervous excitement at reconnecting with Nadia after so many years.

Simon checked his watch, nodding toward the door. "It's about time. Youssef's waiting outside, ready to whisk us off to meet the team. Shall we?"

Ellie glanced around their room one last time before stepping out. She was grateful for the small, comforting space but felt an undeniable pull toward the desert beyond

Amman's bustling streets. Their journey was truly beginning, and the promise of discovering something hidden in the sand felt like a tangible presence.

They descended the narrow staircase of the guesthouse, where Youssef was waiting outside with his ever-present smile. "Good morning, Dr. Ellie, Dr. Simon!" he greeted them warmly. "Are you ready for your first day on site?"

"More than ready," Ellie replied, beaming. "We've been waiting for this."

Youssef drove them through the early morning streets of Amman, which were already buzzing with activity. The golden light softened the cityscape, and Ellie found herself entranced by the view as they moved from the bustle of the city into the sprawling, sun-drenched expanse of the desert.

After about an hour, Youssef slowed the car as they approached a small cluster of tents and vehicles surrounded by a few scattered figures. The dig site was situated in a sheltered area bordered by low hills and rocky outcrops. The sight filled Ellie with a mix of awe and reverence—this was where ancient secrets lay waiting to be revealed.

As they climbed out of the car, Ellie spotted a tall figure moving briskly toward them, her head wrapped in a light scarf to shield her from the sun. The woman wore a rugged, sun-bleached hat and had an air of quiet authority. Her face broke into a warm smile as she drew near.

"Ellie!" she called, her voice full of warmth and familiarity. "It's been too long."

Ellie's face lit up as she recognized Dr. Nadia al-Masri. "Nadia! I can't believe it's really you," Ellie replied, moving forward to clasp Nadia's hand in both of hers. The two women shared a moment, a mutual respect and camaraderie passing between them that bridged the years since they'd last met.

Simon extended his hand, smiling. "Nadia, it's an honor to finally meet you in person. Ellie has spoken so highly of you."

Nadia laughed, shaking Simon's hand warmly. "And I've heard wonderful things about you both. I can't believe you've come all this way to join our little adventure." Her eyes sparkled with a mix of excitement and mischief. "I have a feeling this will be a dig to remember."

She turned to gesture toward a nearby tent, where a young woman was organizing a stack of papers. "This is Layla, my assistant and right hand on the dig. She's as dedicated as they come and has an instinct for uncovering hidden details."

Layla looked up, her dark eyes filled with curiosity and warmth as she approached. She was young, likely in her mid-twenties, with a confident demeanor and an expression that radiated enthusiasm.

"It's an honor to meet you both," Layla said, smiling as she shook hands with Ellie and Simon. "Dr. Whitcombe, I've read your work. It's been a huge inspiration to me. I can't believe I'm getting to work alongside you!"

Ellie felt a surge of pride and gratitude. "Thank you, Layla. That means so much to me. I have a feeling we'll make some exciting discoveries together."

Layla nodded eagerly, and Nadia gestured toward another figure who was standing at a distance, surveying the desert horizon with a practiced gaze. He was tall and lean, with sun-weathered skin and an air of quiet confidence. He wore a traditional keffiyeh, a red-and-white checked scarf that shaded his neck and shoulders from the harsh desert sun.

"This is Amir," Nadia explained. "He's our local guide, and there's no one more knowledgeable about these lands. Amir's expertise has saved us more than once."

Amir approached them with a respectful nod, his eyes keen and observant. "Welcome to Jordan," he said, his voice calm and steady. "It is an honor to guide you through this land. The desert holds many secrets, but it also demands respect."

Simon extended a hand, and Amir shook it, his grip firm and steady. "Thank you, Amir. We're grateful for your guidance."

Amir inclined his head. "The desert can be unforgiving. But with care, it will reveal its truths."

Ellie felt a thrill run through her at his words. There was something about Amir that exuded wisdom, as if he himself had been shaped by the land around them, molded by its rugged beauty and ancient mysteries.

Nadia clapped her hands together, drawing their attention back to her. "Well, now that introductions are made, let's get you acquainted with our work here." She gestured toward the central tent, where a large table was covered with maps, sketches, and a few carefully labeled artifacts. "This is our operations tent. It's where we meet every morning to review our progress and plan out the day's work."

As they gathered around the table, Nadia handed Ellie and Simon a set of sketches depicting the layout of the dig site. "Our main area of focus," Nadia explained, pointing to a spot marked on the map, "is here, where we believe the remains of a Nabatean temple are located. However, we've also found evidence that suggests an even older layer beneath it—possibly from a culture that predates the Nabateans."

Ellie leaned over the map, her heart racing with excitement. "An older layer? That could mean this site was a place of significance long before the Nabateans arrived."

Nadia nodded. "Exactly. That's why this dig is so important. We're not just uncovering a temple; we may be uncovering an entire history that has been hidden for centuries."

Layla joined them, her face filled with excitement. "We've already found a few artifacts—ceramic fragments, ancient tools—that suggest a range of activities took place here. Each day, we're piecing together a bit more of the story."

Simon studied the artifacts, his eyes alight with curiosity. "You're right—this place has layers of history. If these tools are as old as they seem, we could be looking at the lives of people who inhabited this region before anyone ever dreamed of the Nabateans."

Ellie could feel the infectious energy of the team, a shared sense of purpose that bound them together. Here, in the quiet expanse of the desert, they were united by a common goal: to reveal the secrets buried beneath the sands.

Just then, Amir re-entered the tent, carrying a weathered notebook. "I've prepared our routes for today," he announced, placing the notebook on the table. "We'll begin near the main dig site and work our way outward. The sand can be unpredictable, so we'll proceed carefully."

Nadia looked at Ellie and Simon, her expression serious. "I want to stress the importance of safety out here. The desert is a powerful force, and it can be challenging to navigate. We stick together, we keep communication open, and we respect the land."

Ellie nodded, feeling the gravity of her words. This was no casual endeavor; they were stepping into a land that held its own rules, its own dangers. She glanced at Simon, who gave her a reassuring smile. They had spent years exploring together, but there was something different about this place—a rawness, an ancient energy that demanded respect.

As they gathered their equipment, Layla handed Ellie a sun hat and a scarf to shield her from the heat. "You'll need this," she said with a grin. "The sun is relentless out here, and it's easy to lose track of time when you're absorbed in the work."

Ellie thanked her, slipping on the hat and wrapping the scarf loosely around her neck. Simon adjusted his own hat, tucking a small notebook into his pocket, ready to jot down any observations he made throughout the day.

With Amir leading the way, they made their way out of the tent and toward the dig site. The morning sun was already strong, casting long shadows across the sand. As they walked, Amir pointed out subtle signs in the landscape—a particular way the sand had shifted, a scattering of rocks that hinted at ancient structures lying just beneath the surface.

"It's incredible," Ellie murmured to Simon as they followed Amir's lead. "Every step we take feels like we're walking through history."

Simon nodded, his expression thoughtful. "It's a reminder of how connected everything is. The people who lived here, their lives, their stories—it's all still here, preserved in the land."

They reached the main dig site, where a group of researchers and students were carefully excavating a section of exposed stone. The atmosphere was one of focused excitement, each team member handling the ancient stones and artifacts with reverence. Nadia introduced Ellie and Simon to a few of the team members, each one as passionate and dedicated as the next.

"Every artifact we find, every layer we uncover, adds to the story," Nadia explained. "It's a slow process, but it's worth it. This isn't just about archaeology—it's about understanding the lives of people who lived thousands of years ago."

Ellie felt a deep sense of purpose settle over her. She could see it in the faces of everyone around her, a shared respect for the work they were doing and the lives they were uncovering. It was a reminder that history was not just about dates and events—it was about people, about connection.

As they began their work, Ellie and Simon fell easily into the rhythm of the team, each of them focused on a small section of the dig. Hours passed in a peaceful silence, broken only by the occasional murmurs of excitement when a new artifact was unearthed.

By midday, they took a break under the shade of the tent, sipping cool water and sharing stories. Ellie was captivated by Layla's enthusiasm, by Amir's quiet wisdom, and by Nadia's unwavering dedication to the dig. She could see the bond forming between them, a team united by a shared dream.

As the sun began to dip lower in the sky, casting a warm golden glow across the desert, Ellie glanced at Simon, who was documenting their work with his camera. His eyes met hers, a spark of excitement passing between them.

They had come seeking adventure, and here, in the heart of the Jordanian desert, surrounded by passionate allies and the promise of ancient secrets, they had found it.

IMPRESSIONS AND CLUES

The following morning, Ellie and Simon made their way to the dig site with a renewed sense of excitement. Their introduction to the team the previous day had left them buzzing with anticipation, eager to see firsthand what secrets the desert might reveal. They'd sensed from Nadia's enthusiasm that this dig was special, but she hadn't yet shared the full extent of what they might be uncovering.

When they arrived at the operations tent, Nadia was already waiting, standing beside a large table covered in artifacts, notes, and a few worn, ancient-looking maps. Her eyes brightened as she saw Ellie and Simon.

"Good morning! I'm glad you're both here early," Nadia greeted, her voice infused with excitement. "I thought it was time to give you a closer look at what we're dealing with here. This dig holds more questions than answers, and I think you'll find it as fascinating as I do."

Ellie felt her heart race as she took in the array of items spread across the table, each piece a potential clue to a story waiting to be uncovered. "We're eager to learn," she said, glancing at Simon, who was equally captivated.

Nadia pointed to a worn tablet at the center of the table, its surface lined with intricate carvings that seemed to tell a story—one shrouded in mystery. "This particular artifact has been a puzzle for us," Nadia explained. "These symbols don't match anything we've seen in the Nabatean or any known culture in this region. They're faintly recognizable, yet somehow... foreign."

Ellie leaned in, studying the tablet closely. The carvings were worn from centuries of weathering, but she could still make out lines and shapes that seemed deliberately patterned. "It's as if they're speaking a language we almost understand," she murmured, tracing a faint line in the air over the markings. "Some symbols look vaguely familiar, but others are entirely alien."

"That's what makes this piece so intriguing," Nadia replied. "We're still researching the origin, but I believe the tablet holds a message. Whoever created it was communicating something, a narrative or perhaps even instructions, but in a language we haven't fully deciphered."

Simon tilted his head, studying the symbols from a different angle. "Could it be a form of hybrid script? Maybe an intentional blend of languages from different cultures?"

Nadia nodded. "That's one possibility. This region was a cultural crossroads for centuries, with traders and travelers passing through from different lands. If we're looking at a site that served as a meeting point, it could explain why we're seeing elements that don't fully align with any one culture."

Ellie felt a thrill at the idea. "So this place could be more than just a temple or shrine. It might have been a gathering site, a sanctuary where people came together, sharing ideas and beliefs."

"Exactly," Nadia replied, her expression serious. "This dig isn't just about finding artifacts. It's about piecing together a narrative that may have been buried intentionally, one that could expand our understanding of ancient interactions."

Layla joined them, her eyes shining with excitement as she set down a notebook filled with sketches and notes. "We've already started documenting every inch of the site, every artifact," she said. "Each item seems to connect to a larger story, as if the people here were deliberately preserving something significant. This tablet, in particular, feels like it holds a key."

Ellie's gaze lingered on the tablet, the symbols weaving together in a complex pattern. It felt almost alive, as if it held a hidden message just waiting to be revealed. She exchanged a glance with Simon, whose eyes mirrored her excitement.

"What about the rest of the site?" Simon asked, glancing at the maps and sketches. "Are there other areas that might offer clues to what's happening here?"

Nadia nodded, her face turning serious. "There is. There's something I haven't shown you yet." She motioned for them to follow her to a small clearing where a trench had been carefully excavated, revealing a section of wall partially buried beneath layers of sediment and rock.

"This wall was one of our first discoveries," Nadia explained, gesturing toward the exposed stone. "We believe it's a structure that predates the rest of the site, possibly part of an even older complex that this temple was built on top of."

Ellie stepped closer, her gaze sweeping over the wall. The stones were rough-hewn, smoothed by time and weather, and etched with faint carvings. They were too eroded to be fully legible, but she could make out hints of the same symbols she'd seen on the tablet.

"It's incredible," Ellie whispered. "These carvings—are they related to the tablet's symbols?"

Nadia nodded. "Yes, though they're even harder to interpret due to their age and the erosion. But there's more. We used ground-penetrating radar, and it's revealed something intriguing. Behind this wall, there appears to be a hollow space, a chamber or perhaps a passageway that leads somewhere deeper."

Simon's eyes lit up. "So there's a chance that behind this wall, we might find something intact—something untouched."

Layla, who had been watching their expressions, chimed in. "It's possible. This chamber could have been sealed off intentionally, maybe as a protective measure. Whatever is behind that wall could hold clues about the people who built this place and what they valued."

Ellie's heart raced at the thought of entering a sealed chamber that might have remained hidden for centuries. The idea of unearthing objects or symbols that had been left untouched was a thrilling, almost sacred notion.

"So, when do we begin?" Ellie asked, barely able to contain her excitement.

Nadia's lips curved into a smile, her eyes reflecting the same anticipation. "We'll begin excavating carefully tomorrow. I wanted to wait until everyone was here, until we could approach this with the respect and caution it deserves. This isn't just about unearthing artifacts—it's about entering a part of history that's been waiting to be discovered."

They spent the rest of the morning preparing the necessary equipment and documenting the site. Ellie and Simon took detailed notes, photographing the wall from various angles and sketching out the symbols that lined the stones. Each mark felt deliberate, as though the hands that had carved them knew they were creating something that would endure.

Around midday, they gathered for a brief break, taking shelter under a shaded area where water and simple refreshments had been set up. Amir joined them, his presence a calming counterpoint to the excitement swirling around them.

Ellie, who had been studying a worn piece of pottery, looked up at him. "Amir, what do you think this place was used for? Do you have any thoughts on why it might have been hidden so carefully?"

Amir considered her question for a moment, his gaze distant as if he were seeing beyond the present, into the desert's history. "The desert is a place of mystery, of power," he said slowly. "People come to it seeking answers, clarity, or protection. Sometimes, they hide things here not because they are meant to be forgotten, but because they are meant to be found by those who are ready."

Ellie felt a shiver run down her spine at his words. There was a weight to them, a sense of something ancient and wise. She glanced at Simon, who looked equally moved.

"What do you think is behind that wall, Amir?" Simon asked, his voice quiet.

Amir's gaze was steady as he replied, "I think that whatever is there has been waiting for us. The desert does not reveal its secrets easily, but when it does, it chooses carefully."

They fell into a contemplative silence, each of them feeling the weight of Amir's words. Ellie felt a surge of gratitude for being part of this team, for the chance to be part of something that felt larger than life.

When the afternoon heat began to wane, they returned to the wall and continued their documentation, making sure every detail was captured before they started the delicate work of excavation the following day.

As the sun dipped lower in the sky, casting a warm, golden glow across the site, Ellie found herself drawn once more to the tablet, still resting on the table where Nadia had placed it. She traced a finger over the intricate carvings, feeling a strange pull—a sense that the tablet held a key to something much larger than any of them realized.

Simon joined her, his voice barely above a whisper. "What do you think this all means, Ellie? What do you think we're about to find?"

Ellie shook her head, a mix of excitement and trepidation bubbling up inside her. "I don't know, but it feels like we're on the edge of something extraordinary. Whatever lies behind that wall, I have a feeling it will challenge everything we know."

Nadia joined them, her expression one of quiet resolve. "Tomorrow, we'll break through. But we'll do it with care. This isn't just about finding artifacts—it's about understanding a way of life, a set of beliefs that may have been lost to history."

They stood together, gazing at the wall, each of them feeling the anticipation build as the day drew to a close. There was an unspoken understanding between them—a sense that this dig was no ordinary excavation, but a journey into a part of history that had been waiting for them.

As they prepared to head back to camp for the night, Nadia's voice broke the silence. "Tomorrow,

we'll take our first step into the unknown. And whatever we find... I have a feeling it will be something we've never encountered before."

Ellie felt a thrill at her words, and as they walked back together under the desert sky, she knew she wouldn't be able to sleep. Tomorrow, they would cross the threshold into a hidden world, one that had waited centuries to be rediscovered.

And for the first time, Ellie felt certain that the desert had chosen them.

THE UNEXPECTED DISCOVERY

The morning sun was still low in the sky as Ellie, Simon, and the rest of the team gathered near the wall where they'd begin their excavation. The air was cool, yet tinged with an underlying heat that promised to intensify as the day wore on. Tools lay neatly arranged beside them, and a sense of anticipation hummed through the group, making the atmosphere feel charged.

Nadia looked around at the team, her expression resolute. "Today, we'll start carefully removing the stones along this section of the wall. Our goal is to expose whatever chamber lies behind it without damaging the structure. Every move must be measured. This isn't just about finding artifacts—it's about respecting what's hidden within."

Ellie felt a thrill as she nodded in agreement. There was something almost sacred about this process, as if they were entering a space that had been waiting patiently to reveal its secrets. She glanced at Simon, who returned her gaze with the same mix of excitement and reverence.

The work was painstaking. The team took turns chiseling away small sections of stone, easing them from the wall's grip. Hours passed, and the sounds of scraping and shifting filled the air. Layla worked alongside Ellie, her youthful enthusiasm tempered by focus and care as she removed each piece of rock.

Finally, after what felt like an eternity, they exposed a narrow passageway leading deeper into the earth. The team peered into the opening, their flashlights casting beams that barely penetrated the inky darkness beyond.

"This is it," Layla whispered, her voice filled with awe. "We're about to step into something untouched for centuries."

Nadia moved forward, her flashlight illuminating the passageway. "Let's proceed carefully. Layla, Amir, Ellie, and Simon, you'll come with me. The rest of the team will stay here and continue documenting."

They slipped through the narrow opening, one by one, descending down a short, steep staircase carved into the stone. The air grew cool and dense as they moved deeper, the walls pressing in around them. Each step felt like a descent into another time, a journey into a world that had been hidden for generations.

When they reached the bottom of the staircase, the passageway opened into a small, low-ceilinged chamber. The walls were covered in a series of faint carvings, symbols and patterns that seemed to flow and connect in an intricate web. Ellie felt her heart pound as she took in the carvings, each line and curve etched with purpose.

"Look at this," she murmured, her voice barely above a whisper. "These symbols—they're different from anything we've seen on the other artifacts."

Nadia nodded, her eyes scanning the walls. "Yes, they're distinct. And they're arranged in sequences, almost like a narrative or code. It's as if they're telling a story."

Ellie ran her fingers over a section of the wall, feeling the rough texture beneath her touch. The symbols seemed familiar, yet foreign, a blend of patterns that hinted at an ancient language. She could make out circles, spirals, and interlocking shapes, each one flowing seamlessly into the next.

Layla's eyes gleamed with excitement as she examined the carvings. "These symbols remind me of ancient pictograms I've studied. But they're more complex—almost like they're blending ideas rather than just depicting objects or events."

Amir, who had been studying a particularly elaborate section of the wall, turned to Layla. "What do you make of these carvings, Layla? Could they be connected to the lost kingdoms we've only read about in myths?"

Layla's face lit up, and she moved closer to the wall, her hands almost trembling with excitement. "It's possible. There are theories that certain ancient kingdoms existed in this region long before recorded history, empires that thrived and then disappeared without a trace. If that's true, then this site might be the first evidence of such a civilization."

Simon's eyes narrowed as he studied the symbols. "So we could be looking at a kingdom that vanished, a civilization whose existence was erased."

Layla nodded enthusiastically. "Exactly. There's a theory about a lost kingdom called Iram of the Pillars, a city that vanished in the sands. Some believe it was more than a city—that it was a powerful empire. Legends say it was known for its knowledge and wealth, but it disappeared, swallowed by the desert, leaving no trace behind."

Ellie felt a chill as Layla spoke. She'd heard stories of lost kingdoms and cities buried beneath the sands, tales of civilizations that had thrived and then faded into legend. But hearing Layla describe it here, in the shadowed depths of an ancient chamber, made it feel almost real.

"These symbols," Layla continued, her fingers tracing a series of spirals, "could be an early form of language. If this is Iram or a place like it, then we might be looking at a form of writing unique to that culture, a language that's never been recorded."

Nadia's expression grew thoughtful. "This would be one of the most significant finds of our time if we can link these symbols to a lost kingdom. It would reshape our understanding of this region's history."

Amir, who had been silent, spoke softly, his gaze fixed on a particular section of the wall. "The desert guards its secrets well, but sometimes, it allows us a glimpse. If these symbols are indeed part of a lost language, then perhaps this site was meant to preserve that knowledge, to pass it down to those who are willing to listen."

Ellie glanced at Amir, sensing a deep respect in his voice. There was a sense of reverence that connected them all, a shared understanding that they were standing on sacred ground, unearthing something that had been preserved with purpose.

They continued to examine the symbols, documenting each section with photographs and sketches. Layla's excitement was contagious, her voice filled with theories as she speculated on the possible meanings behind the shapes and patterns.

"Look at this section," Layla said, pointing to a series of interconnected spirals. "Spirals often represent cycles—birth, life, death, and rebirth. It's possible these symbols are meant to depict a journey, a passage through different stages or realms."

Ellie's gaze drifted over the spirals, her mind racing with possibilities. "A spiritual journey, perhaps? Maybe this chamber was meant as a place for rituals, a sacred space where people could connect with the divine."

Simon joined them, his camera capturing every detail. "If this chamber was indeed used for rituals, it would explain why it was hidden so carefully. The people who built this place might have considered it sacred, reserved only for those who understood its purpose."

They moved to another section of the wall, where a series of geometric patterns caught Ellie's attention. Unlike the spirals, these shapes were sharp and angular, each one intricately connected to the next.

"These look almost like constellations," she observed. "Could they be a map of the stars?"

Layla's face lit up with recognition. "Yes! I was just thinking that. Many ancient cultures used star maps as part of their spiritual practices. If this civilization was as advanced as the legends suggest, they could have developed their own form of astrology, using the stars to guide their rituals."

Nadia's voice was filled with awe as she spoke. "If that's true, then we're not just looking at a religious site—we're looking at a culture that had a profound understanding of astronomy and the cosmos. They might have seen themselves as part of a larger, universal story."

Ellie felt a sense of wonder settle over her as she absorbed Nadia's words. The idea that these people had used the stars to connect with something beyond themselves, to understand their place in the universe, was humbling. She felt as though they were glimpsing a part of history that transcended time, a piece of humanity that had been lost but was now coming back to light.

Just then, Simon, who had moved to the far end of the chamber, called out, his voice echoing off the stone walls. "Ellie, Nadia, Layla—come look at this!"

They hurried over to where he was standing, his flashlight illuminating a small alcove carved into the wall. Inside the alcove lay an object, partially covered in dust. Ellie's heart raced as she reached out, carefully brushing away the dirt to reveal what appeared to be a small, intricately carved stone disc.

Layla gasped, her eyes wide with astonishment. "I've never seen anything like this."

The disc was covered in symbols similar to those on the walls, but they were arranged in a circular pattern, radiating outward from the center. At the heart of the disc was a single, spiral symbol, larger and more deeply carved than the others.

"It's beautiful," Ellie whispered, her fingers hovering over the disc. "But what could it mean?"

Nadia examined it closely, her expression thoughtful. "It could be a ritual object, perhaps used in ceremonies or as part of some ancient belief system. The spiral at the center—it's almost like a focal point, as if it represents something central to their beliefs."

Amir, who had been observing quietly, spoke up. "In some ancient traditions, the spiral represents the journey inward, a path to self-discovery. It's possible this disc was used to guide people on their spiritual journey, a way to connect with their inner selves or the divine."

Ellie's mind raced with the possibilities. This object wasn't just a relic—it was

a piece of an ancient worldview, a glimpse into the minds and hearts of people who had walked these lands long before recorded history.

As they continued examining the disc, a sense of awe filled the chamber. They were no longer just archaeologists uncovering artifacts; they were explorers stepping into a forgotten world, piecing together fragments of a culture that had been lost to time.

"Let's take this back to the operations tent and examine it in more detail," Nadia said, carefully placing the disc into a padded case. "This could be a key to understanding the symbols here—and perhaps to discovering more about who these people were."

Ellie nodded, but a lingering feeling tugged at her. There was more to this chamber, more secrets hidden in the carvings, the symbols, the air itself. As they prepared to leave, she couldn't shake the feeling that this discovery was only the beginning, that the desert had far more to reveal.

As they filed back through the passageway, climbing up the stone steps to the surface, Ellie's heart raced with anticipation. They'd uncovered something extraordinary, something that held echoes of a lost kingdom, a vanished civilization that had left its mark in symbols and stone.

And as they emerged into the light, she knew that this was just the start of a journey that would challenge everything they knew about history, about humanity, and perhaps even about themselves.

KARIM'S ARRIVAL

The day following the team's discovery of the chamber was filled with analysis, documentation, and discussions that lingered well into the night. Ellie and Simon, along with the rest of the team, were still reeling from the implications of the stone disc they'd found and the intricate symbols adorning the chamber walls. Layla was particularly animated, filling pages of her notebook with theories and sketches as they dissected every angle of the find.

The excitement was palpable, a shared thrill that permeated every conversation, every glance exchanged. But as the morning sun rose over the desert, casting a warm glow across the dig site, an unexpected visitor arrived, casting a shadow over their newfound excitement.

Ellie noticed him first—a tall man standing just beyond the perimeter of the site, watching them with a casual yet piercing gaze. Dressed in a crisp white shirt and dark slacks, he seemed out of place among the dusty tents and rugged landscape. His eyes, sharp and calculating, surveyed the team's movements with an unsettling intensity.

"Nadia," Ellie said, gesturing subtly toward the figure. "Who's that?"

Nadia's expression darkened as she followed Ellie's gaze. "Karim. I wasn't expecting him so soon."

"Who is he?" Simon asked, picking up on Nadia's change in demeanor.

"A journalist," Nadia replied, though there was a note of reluctance in her voice. "He's well-known in certain circles for his interest in archaeological finds, but his reputation is... complicated. He covers high-profile digs, usually ones involving significant discoveries. But he's known to have connections beyond just journalism."

Ellie frowned, sensing an undercurrent in Nadia's words. "What do you mean?"

Nadia hesitated, her gaze fixed on Karim as he approached. "Let's just say Karim isn't always interested in history for history's sake. He's drawn to sites where valuable artifacts might be found. There are rumors he's associated with individuals who see these relics as commodities rather than pieces of heritage."

As Karim neared, he offered a polite, almost charming smile, though his eyes held a keen edge. "Dr. Nadia al-

Masri," he greeted, his voice smooth. "It's a pleasure, as always."

Nadia's response was measured, her tone polite yet distant. "Karim, I wasn't expecting you this soon. We're still in the early stages of our work here."

Karim's smile widened. "I couldn't resist. Word has it you're uncovering some interesting pieces—a hidden chamber, ancient carvings, perhaps even lost artifacts?"

His gaze shifted to Ellie and Simon, his eyes narrowing with a subtle, appraising gleam. "And you must be the Whitcombes, the couple who traveled all the way from New York to join this dig. Quite the adventure, isn't it?"

Ellie felt an instinctual unease settle over her, a warning in the back of her mind. She forced a polite smile. "Yes, we're thrilled to be here. The discoveries have been fascinating."

Karim's smile didn't reach his eyes as he regarded her. "I imagine they have. A site like this—there's so much potential, don't you think? So much history buried beneath the sand, just waiting to be unearthed."

He said the words with a faint, lingering tone that suggested he saw the site through a different lens, one focused more on value than history.

Nadia, ever the professional, kept her tone steady. "Karim, if you're interested in covering the dig, we'll be happy to arrange a time for you to document our findings. However, we're keeping things quiet until we have more definitive information."

Karim's smile turned wry, his gaze flickering back to Ellie and Simon. "Of course, discretion is key," he said smoothly. "But I must admit, I've developed a rather personal interest in this dig. You see, the rumors I've heard suggest there's something quite special here—something with a value that goes beyond mere historical interest."

Simon, ever the steady presence, responded calmly. "We're here to uncover history, Karim. Each artifact and symbol tells a story that goes beyond monetary value. That's what we're focused on."

Karim's eyes lingered on Simon for a moment, his expression unreadable. "Indeed, Dr. Whitcombe. But I've found that history and value often go hand in hand. And some stories... well, they're worth a great deal to the right buyer."

Ellie felt a chill at his words, and a spark of anger flared within her. It was clear that Karim saw this site not as a repository of cultural heritage, but as an opportunity—a vault of treasures waiting to be claimed. She glanced at Nadia, whose gaze had hardened, a subtle but firm warning directed at Karim.

"Karim," Nadia said evenly, her voice carrying a subtle edge, "this dig is not open for... outside speculation. We're committed to preserving and studying the artifacts we uncover, not selling them to the highest bidder."

Karim chuckled, feigning innocence. "Dr. al-Masri, you misunderstand me. I'm merely here to observe, to document, and perhaps to share the significance of your work with the world. After all, what good is history if it remains hidden?"

There was an unspoken tension in the air, an acknowledgment of the different values that each of them placed on the dig. Karim's gaze shifted again to Ellie, his eyes narrowing with something that felt almost like a challenge.

"You seem like someone who understands the value of knowledge, Dr. Whitcombe," he said, his tone almost conspiratorial. "Imagine what people would pay to possess pieces of history like the ones you're uncovering here. Not everyone has the opportunity to be here, after all. Some would give anything to hold such treasures in their hands."

Ellie bristled, sensing the insinuation behind his words. She held his gaze, her voice steady but firm. "Our goal is to preserve history, Karim, not sell it. Each artifact belongs to the culture it came from, to the people who walked this land long before us. They're not ours to give away."

Karim's expression didn't falter, but there was a flicker of something dark in his eyes. "Ah, preservation," he said with a soft chuckle. "A noble pursuit. But history, Dr. Whitcombe, is often a matter of perspective. And as time goes on, the lines between preservation and possession can blur."

Simon stepped forward, his tone calm but carrying a clear undertone of resolve. "Perhaps, Karim. But those are lines we intend to keep clear."

For a brief moment, Karim's mask slipped, revealing a flash of irritation. But he quickly recovered, his charming smile returning as he nodded politely. "Of course. I wouldn't dream of interfering with your work. I simply wanted to introduce myself and extend an offer—should you need assistance in... reaching a wider audience."

Nadia's expression remained impassive. "Thank you for the offer, Karim. We'll let you know if we require any additional coverage."

Karim took the hint, inclining his head with a mock-politeness. "I'll leave you to your work, then. But don't hesitate to reach out. After all, we're all here to uncover the truth, aren't we?"

He turned and walked away, his footsteps crunching softly in the sand as he disappeared beyond the tents. The team watched him go, a sense of unease settling over them like a shadow.

Ellie let out a breath she hadn't realized she was holding. "Well... that was unsettling," she murmured.

Nadia nodded, her gaze still fixed on the direction Karim had taken. "That's Karim. Always charming, always calculating. I've known him for years, and I can tell you that his interest in archaeology is more transactional than historical. He has connections to people who view artifacts as assets, not heritage."

Layla, who had been listening quietly, looked troubled. "Do you think he's here because of what we found yesterday? The disc and the symbols?"

Nadia's expression darkened. "Possibly. News of significant finds spreads quickly in this world. And Karim... he's always tuned in, especially when there's the potential for profit."

Ellie felt a knot of worry tighten in her stomach. She'd encountered passionate people in her field, individuals who saw history as a source of knowledge and legacy. But Karim's presence reminded her that archaeology also had a dark side, one that viewed ancient cultures as nothing more than a source of wealth.

"We'll need to be careful," Simon said quietly, his tone serious. "If he has contacts who are interested in artifacts... he might try to gain more access to the site, or even attempt to disrupt our work."

Nadia nodded, her expression resolute. "We'll double our security. I'll inform the team to keep a close eye on him if he returns. I've seen his type before, and I won't let him interfere with our work here."

Ellie felt a surge of gratitude for Nadia's unwavering dedication. They were here to uncover history, to bring the past to light—not to watch it vanish into private collections.

As the team returned to their work, a lingering unease remained. Karim's arrival had cast a shadow over the dig, a reminder that their work wasn't just about discovery—it was about protection. They were not only archaeologists but guardians of a heritage that had survived for centuries. And now, they would need to guard it from those who would seek to exploit it.

But as they resumed their tasks, Ellie couldn't shake the feeling that Karim's visit was just the beginning. His words echoed in her mind, a subtle warning that something darker lurked beneath the surface of their work, waiting to emerge.

CHAP

8

DANGER DANGER!

The desert had begun to cool as the late afternoon sun dipped closer to the horizon. The day's work had been exhausting but exhilarating, as the team continued their careful examination of the chamber and its enigmatic carvings. The day was winding down, yet Ellie and Simon, ever curious, lingered at the edge of the excavation site, inspecting a smaller, newly uncovered cave section. They had an unshakable feeling that there was more to this place than met the eye.

Ellie knelt down, examining the rocks at the cave's entrance, her fingers brushing away the layers of dust. The air inside was cool and damp, carrying an earthy smell that hinted at years of stillness. She looked over at Simon, her eyes alight with intrigue. "Doesn't it feel like there's something buried here, something hidden just out of sight?"

Simon nodded, sharing her sense of anticipation. "I can feel it too. It's like this place has been waiting for someone to come along and ask the right questions."

They'd both been enchanted by the mysterious carvings in the chamber, and each new discovery only fueled their determination to uncover the truth. With care, they took a few steps inside, their flashlights cutting through the dimness and casting flickering beams along the rugged stone walls.

"Look here," Ellie whispered, pointing to a set of faint etchings on the wall to her right. "It's hard to see, but it almost looks like another set of symbols, maybe older than the ones we've found so far."

Simon leaned in, squinting as he adjusted his flashlight for a better view. The markings were faint, but there was a pattern, a sense of deliberation in each line and curve. "It's strange. They're similar to the other symbols, but rougher, almost as if whoever carved them was working quickly or in secret."

They shared a moment of silent awe, each of them feeling the weight of history pressing in around them. This cave felt ancient, older than the main chamber they'd been exploring. Ellie's mind raced with possibilities—could this section of the site predate even the Nabatean influence? Could it be connected to the fabled lost kingdoms Layla had mentioned?

But before she could voice her thoughts, a faint, unsettling sound echoed through the cave—a low rumble, like distant thunder rolling through the stone. Ellie's heart skipped a beat as she glanced at Simon, her pulse quickening with sudden anxiety.

"Did you hear that?" she whispered, her voice barely audible over the deepening rumble.

Simon's gaze shifted to the cave entrance, his face tense. "Yeah, I heard it. We should move back, just in case."

They turned to leave, but before they could take more than a few steps, the ground beneath them shuddered, and a deafening crack reverberated through the cave. Rocks began to shift, tumbling down from the ceiling as the air filled with dust and debris. Ellie's instincts kicked in, and she grabbed Simon's arm, pulling him toward the entrance.

"Run!" she shouted, her voice muffled by the dust swirling around them.

They stumbled forward, the narrow passage seeming to close in on them as rocks crashed to the ground on either side. Ellie's vision blurred, her lungs straining as she inhaled the dust-laden air. She clung to Simon, their movements frantic as they fought to reach the opening before it was blocked.

Another tremor shook the ground, and Ellie felt the solid weight of a rock brush past her shoulder, narrowly missing her. She gasped, adrenaline surging through her veins as she pushed onward, her entire body focused on escape.

"Almost there!" Simon's voice sounded distant, strained, as he pulled her forward, guiding her through the thickening haze of dust.

Just as they reached the entrance, a final, thunderous crack echoed through the cave, and a massive slab of rock broke free from the ceiling, crashing down mere inches behind them. They stumbled out of the cave, collapsing onto the sand as the air around them settled, and the echoes of the collapse faded into silence.

Ellie lay on the ground, gasping for breath, her body trembling from the shock. She looked over at Simon, relief flooding her as she saw he was unharmed, though his face was streaked with dust and his breathing was as labored as her own.

"Are you okay?" he asked, his voice hoarse.

Ellie nodded, though her heart was still pounding. "I think so. That was... close."

They sat in silence for a moment, the weight of what had just happened settling over them. The cave entrance was now partially blocked, a pile of rocks and debris forming a barrier that would take hours to clear. Ellie's mind raced, trying to process the sudden collapse and the fact that they'd narrowly escaped being trapped—or worse.

As her breathing steadied, a thought struck her, one that sent a chill down her spine. "Simon... that collapse. It didn't feel natural. Did you notice the way it started, the sounds?"

Simon's brow furrowed, and he nodded slowly. "It was strange. There was no warning, no sign of instability in the rock when we first went in. And the rumbling... it almost felt like something triggered it."

A heavy silence fell between them as they exchanged a look of mutual understanding. The possibility was unsettling, but Ellie couldn't shake the feeling that the collapse had been deliberate, as if someone had wanted to trap them inside.

Just then, Layla and Amir came rushing toward them, their faces filled with concern. "Ellie! Simon! Are you alright?" Layla asked, her voice breathless as she surveyed the scene.

"We're fine," Ellie replied, though her voice shook slightly. "We just barely made it out before the collapse."

Without a word, Amir handed them each a canteen of water. Ellie accepted it gratefully, taking a long sip, the coolness soothing her parched throat. The dust she'd swallowed seemed to cling to every surface inside her mouth, but the water brought a refreshing sense of relief. She passed the canteen to Simon, who took his own sip, coughing slightly as he swallowed.

"Thank you," he said, his voice still rough but steadier. He wiped his mouth with the back of his hand, casting a wary glance back at the cave entrance.

Amir's gaze shifted to the cave entrance, his expression darkening. "This is... unusual. That section of the cave was stable. There was no reason for it to collapse like this, especially so suddenly."

Layla's face mirrored his concern, and Ellie could see the wheels turning in her mind. "You don't think... someone could have caused this?" she asked, her voice barely above a whisper.

Ellie hesitated, glancing at Simon, who gave a small nod. "It's possible," she said, her voice steady but filled with unease. "The collapse felt unnatural, almost as if it had been triggered."

Nadia, who had been working nearby, arrived at the scene, her face pale with worry as she looked over the debris blocking the cave. "What happened here?"

Simon explained the collapse, recounting the sudden rumbling and the way the cave had seemed to shift and close in on them. Nadia listened intently, her expression growing more serious with every word.

"This doesn't make sense," she said, her tone laced with tension. "That section of the cave has been thoroughly inspected. There were no signs of instability or structural weakness."

Layla glanced over at the blocked entrance, her brow furrowing. "Do you think it could have been sabotage?"

The word hung in the air, heavy and ominous. Ellie felt a shiver run down her spine as she considered the implications. Sabotage? The idea was unsettling, but it made a twisted kind of sense. If someone wanted to interfere with the dig, to stop them from uncovering the site's secrets, a cave collapse would be an effective way to send a message.

Simon voiced what they were all thinking. "Karim. He was here yesterday, showing more interest in the artifacts than in the history itself. He made it clear he values... other aspects of archaeology."

Nadia's eyes darkened, and she crossed her arms, her expression unreadable. "It's possible. Karim has a way of pushing boundaries when it suits his interests. But we have no proof, and he'd deny any involvement."

Amir nodded thoughtfully, his gaze fixed on the cave entrance. "If Karim or someone associated with him did this, they're sending a message—a warning. They want us to know they're watching."

A sense of unease settled over the group, the weight of the situation pressing down on them. They had come here to uncover history, to piece together a forgotten narrative. But now, they were faced with the possibility that their work was being actively sabotaged, that someone saw this dig as a threat.

Ellie clenched her fists, anger rising within her. They couldn't let someone like Karim derail their work, couldn't let him taint the integrity of what they were doing. This dig was about preservation, about bringing the past to light—not about profit or possession.

"What are we going to do?" Layla asked, her voice filled with determination.

Nadia's expression was resolute. "We're going to continue. This site is too important to abandon, and we won't be intimidated by threats. But we'll need to be vigilant. If Karim or anyone else tries to interfere again, we'll be ready."

Ellie felt a surge of admiration for Nadia's courage, her unshakable commitment to the dig. They were here for a purpose, one that went beyond artifacts and history. They were here to protect the legacy of the people who had come before them, to honor their stories.

As the team regrouped, making plans to reinforce the site's security and ensure that all entrances were monitored, Ellie found herself glancing back at the blocked cave. The narrow escape had left her shaken, but it had also strengthened her resolve. She and Simon had come here to uncover the truth, and no amount of intimidation would stop them from pursuing that goal.

After a final debrief in the communal tent where they discussed plans to increase security, Ellie and Simon packed up their equipment and made their way to the car. As they drove back to their apartment, the desert landscape unfurled around them, both beautiful and silent, holding its secrets close.

Once back at their apartment, Simon reached for her hand, giving it a reassuring squeeze. "We'll get through this," he said softly. "No matter what they try to throw at us, we'll see this through."

Ellie nodded, her gaze steady. "We will. They can try to scare us, but they don't know who they're dealing with."

They shared a quiet smile, a shared understanding passing between them. This dig was no longer just an archaeological expedition—it had become a fight to preserve the truth, to protect the stories that had been buried for centuries.

As they settled in for the night, Ellie couldn't shake the feeling that the danger wasn't over, that the collapse was only the beginning. But she pushed the fear aside, focusing instead on the task ahead. They were standing at the edge of something extraordinary, something worth fighting for. And no one, not even Karim, would keep them from uncovering the mysteries hidden in the desert sands.

A PROFESSOR'S INSIGHT

The next morning, Ellie and Simon made their way into the bustling heart of Amman, the city stretching and unfurling with the morning sun. Today, they were visiting Professor Malik Ibrahim, a respected historian at the University of Jordan who specialized in Near Eastern symbols and cultures. They'd heard of his expertise from Nadia, who assured them that Malik's insight could be invaluable in interpreting the symbols they'd found.

As their taxi wound through Amman's lively streets, Ellie and Simon marveled at the contrasts around them. Traditional markets stood side-by-side with modern buildings, and the ancient city walls seemed to meld effortlessly with contemporary architecture. Amman felt like a bridge between worlds—just as their work was a bridge between the past and the present.

"Do you think Malik will have answers for us?" Ellie asked, glancing over at Simon, who was reviewing some of the sketches they'd made of the cave's symbols.

"If anyone will, it's him," Simon replied. "From what Nadia told us, Malik is one of the foremost experts in ancient Jordanian cultures and languages. If these symbols are part of an older language or ritual, he'll recognize it."

They arrived at the university, where they were met by a guide who led them through the sprawling campus. The buildings were a mix of traditional stonework and sleek modern designs, blending seamlessly into the landscape. Their guide brought them to an office lined with books, scrolls, and artifacts—Professor Malik Ibrahim's domain.

As they entered, an older man with silver hair and sharp, discerning eyes rose to greet them. He wore a traditional Jordanian robe beneath his academic blazer, a blend of heritage and modernity that matched his surroundings.

"Dr. Whitcombe, Dr. Whitcombe," he greeted warmly, shaking both their hands. "Welcome to my humble office. Nadia has told me much about you, and it's an honor to have you here."

"The honor is ours, Professor Malik," Ellie replied with a smile. "We're very grateful for your time and expertise."

Malik gestured for them to sit, his gaze settling on the folder of sketches Simon was holding. "I understand you've come across some rather unusual symbols in your dig. Nadia mentioned that they're unlike anything you've encountered before?"

Ellie nodded, handing him the folder. "Yes. The carvings seem distinct from the Nabatean symbols we're familiar with, and they don't match any known language or pattern we've studied. We were hoping you could shed some light on their origin."

Malik opened the folder and began studying the sketches intently. For a long moment, he was silent, his brow furrowing in concentration. Then he looked up, his expression serious.

"These are... interesting," he said slowly. "They contain elements of known languages, yet they appear to be more symbolic, almost ritualistic in nature."

"Ritualistic?" Simon repeated, intrigued. "Do you mean they could be part of a ceremonial practice?"

Malik nodded. "Yes. From my studies, I've found that ancient cultures in this region often used symbols not only to communicate but to invoke protection, guidance, or blessings. The spiral and circular patterns here, for example, could represent the cycle of life, a common theme in spiritual practices."

Ellie leaned forward, captivated. "We found these symbols in a hidden chamber, deep within a cave. They were arranged in sequences, almost like a narrative. Do you think they could be part of a story, or even a ritual journey?"

Malik's eyes gleamed with excitement. "It's very possible. Certain ancient communities believed that spiritual knowledge had to be earned, that one's journey through life was a form of initiation. A hidden chamber such as the one you've described could have been a sacred space, a place where individuals connected with the divine through symbols and rituals."

The idea sent a thrill through Ellie. She'd always sensed a purpose behind the symbols, an intentionality that went beyond mere decoration. But hearing Malik's interpretation gave new weight to their discoveries.

Simon, who had been listening intently, asked, "Are there specific cultures in Jordanian history that would have used such symbols? Iram of the Pillars, perhaps? Layla mentioned a theory about lost kingdoms that may have influenced this region."

Malik considered the question, his gaze drifting to the shelves lined with historical texts. "Iram of the Pillars is a fascinating theory, though there is little concrete evidence to confirm its existence. But legends of lost kingdoms often contain fragments of truth, and if such a place did exist, it may have influenced neighboring cultures, passing on its knowledge through oral traditions and symbols."

He paused, his gaze turning serious. "You see, Jordan was a cultural crossroads for centuries. This land was not only home to the Nabateans but to countless other groups—travelers, traders, refugees—all of whom left their mark. It's entirely possible that the symbols you've found are remnants of a lost culture that thrived here before history as we know it was recorded."

Ellie's mind raced with the implications. "So, if we could decipher these symbols, we might be looking at a glimpse into a culture that existed long before our historical records?"

"Precisely," Malik replied, his voice filled with reverence. "And that's why this dig is so significant. But I must caution you," he added, his tone turning somber. "The stakes here are higher than you might realize."

Ellie felt a prickle of unease. "What do you mean?"

Malik leaned forward, folding his hands as he spoke. "In this part of the world, artifacts are not just objects—they are pieces of history, heritage, and identity. They connect us to our ancestors, to the land, and to each other. But not everyone sees them this way. There are those who view these artifacts as commodities, things to be bought, sold, or traded."

Simon's face hardened, and Ellie knew he was thinking of Karim. "We've encountered someone like that," he said quietly. "A journalist named Karim. He seemed more interested in the artifacts' value than their history."

Malik's expression grew grave. "Karim is well-known in certain circles. He has connections to individuals and groups who deal in the black market for antiquities. It's a dark industry, one that thrives on the theft and exploitation of cultural heritage. If Karim has taken an interest in your dig, you must be vigilant. People in his line of work do not tolerate interference lightly."

Ellie shivered, Malik's words bringing back memories of the cave collapse, the sense that they'd been trapped by something—or someone—intent on halting their progress.

Malik continued, his gaze steady. "You are uncovering artifacts and symbols that may be priceless, not only in monetary value but in cultural significance. Such discoveries attract attention, often from people who have no regard for preservation. The collapse you described... if you suspect foul play, you must take precautions."

Ellie's mind raced with questions, her heart pounding with a mix of excitement and fear. They'd come here to uncover history, to bring lost stories to light. But now, it seemed, they were facing an adversary who would stop at nothing to claim the site's treasures for themselves.

"Professor Malik," she asked hesitantly, "what can we do to protect the site? We can't let this dig be compromised by people who don't respect its heritage."

Malik smiled, though it was tinged with sadness. "I admire your dedication, Ellie. But protecting a site like this is not easy. There are many who would argue that artifacts belong in private collections or museums far from their place of origin. But you can take some steps to safeguard your work. First, keep detailed records of every item you find. Documentation is your ally. Even if artifacts are lost or stolen, a record of their existence and significance will endure."

Simon nodded. "We've been photographing and cataloging everything meticulously. Nadia has set up a secure system, but we'll double our efforts."

"Good," Malik replied. "And be discreet. The fewer people who know the specifics of what you're finding, the safer you'll be. Artifacts that are left undisturbed draw less attention than those that are heralded as 'priceless treasures.'"

Ellie and Simon exchanged a glance, realizing the importance of keeping their discoveries under wraps. They'd always worked transparently, sharing each discovery with their team and, eventually, the academic community. But now, they understood that a level of caution was necessary.

"Thank you, Professor," Ellie said, her voice sincere. "We hadn't realized how high the stakes truly were. Your advice means a lot to us."

Malik inclined his head, his expression thoughtful. "I have one more piece of advice, though it may sound strange. Trust your instincts. In the field of archaeology, knowledge is vital, but intuition often guides us toward truths that logic alone cannot reveal. You and Simon sensed something unusual about this dig, didn't you?"

Ellie felt a chill at his words. "Yes... from the moment we arrived, it felt like this place was calling to us, like there was something waiting to be found."

Malik smiled knowingly. "That is the gift of archaeology. The past speaks to those who are willing to listen. But remember—some voices are meant to remain silent. There are mysteries that the desert has guarded for centuries, and it will not give them up easily."

Ellie nodded, absorbing his words. There was a reverence to Malik's tone, a sense that he understood the desert's secrets better than most. She felt a renewed respect for the dig, a sense of responsibility to honor the land and the people who had come before.

As they prepared to leave, Malik offered them each a small, hand-carved token—a simple piece of sandstone etched with a protective symbol. "These are talismans," he explained. "Symbols of protection passed down through my family. Wear them, and may they bring you safety and wisdom on your journey."

Ellie accepted the talisman with gratitude, touched by Malik's gesture. The small stone felt cool and grounding in her hand, a reminder that they were connected to something larger than themselves.

"Thank you, Professor," she said, her voice filled with emotion. "We'll carry this with us."

Malik nodded, his eyes kind yet solemn. "May your journey be one of discovery, but may it also be one of respect. You are in a place of great power and history. Treat it with care."

As they left the university, Ellie and Simon walked in silence, each of them deep in thought. Malik's words had left a lasting impression, his warnings lingering in their minds. They understood now that the stakes were far greater than they'd realized. This was not just a dig—it was a battle to protect a legacy, a culture, a history that had endured for centuries.

When they returned to their apartment that evening, Ellie hung the talisman around her neck, feeling its reassuring weight. She glanced over at Simon, who was doing the same, their shared commitment evident in the determined look they exchanged.

"Whatever happens," Ellie said softly, "we'll protect this site. We owe it to the people who came before us, and to those who will come after."

Simon nodded, his expression resolute. "Agreed. No one—Karim or anyone else—will take this history away."

They sat together, feeling a renewed sense of purpose as they prepared for the days ahead. Professor Malik's insight had illuminated not only the meaning of the symbols but the importance of their mission. They were protectors of history now, bound to a legacy older than they could imagine.

And as they drifted off to sleep, the desert's silent whispers seemed to echo Malik's words—a reminder that the past was watching, and that they were not alone in their journey.

YOUSSEF'S WARNING

M orning light filtered through the curtains of their apartment, casting soft patterns across the room. Ellie stirred, blinking as she adjusted to the daylight, her mind still lingering on the previous day's revelations. Professor Malik's warnings about the dangers surrounding their dig had weighed heavily on her mind through the night. She turned to find Simon already awake, his gaze fixed on the ceiling, as though lost in his own thoughts.

"You're thinking about it too, aren't you?" she murmured, shifting closer to him.

He turned to her, his expression somber. "It's hard not to. Malik made it clear—we're not just uncovering history; we're protecting it. And with people like Karim around, that's going to take more than careful digging."

They lay in silence for a few moments, absorbing the gravity of their situation. Just then, a soft knock on their door broke the quiet. They exchanged a glance, wondering who it could be at this early hour. Simon got up and opened the door to find Amina, their landlady, standing there with a warm smile and a tray of tea.

"I hope I'm not disturbing you," Amina said, stepping in. "I thought you might like a little refreshment after such a busy day yesterday."

Ellie smiled, grateful for the gesture. "You're too kind, Amina. It was a long day, and we really appreciate this."

Amina set the tray on the small table by the window, her warm eyes lingering on Ellie and Simon. "I know you're both dedicated to your work. And I understand that it is... important." She hesitated, glancing around as if to ensure they were truly alone. "But please, I urge you to be careful. Amman holds many wonders, but not everyone who searches for them does so with respect."

Ellie and Simon exchanged a look, Malik's warnings echoing in Amina's words. Ellie reached out to take her hand. "Thank you, Amina. We're doing everything we can to stay vigilant. Your hospitality means so much to us."

Amina inclined her head, her expression filled with a quiet understanding. "You are welcome here, and I want you to know I am always nearby. Should you ever need help, do not hesitate to call on me." She gave them a reassuring smile before leaving them to their tea.

As they sipped the hot tea, Ellie felt a renewed sense of gratitude for the quiet support they'd found in Amman.

Amina's presence was comforting, a reminder that they were not entirely alone in this unfamiliar world. They finished their tea and were discussing their plans for the day when another knock sounded at the door. This time, it was Youssef.

"Good morning, Ellie, Simon," Youssef greeted, his face a blend of concern and warmth. "I hope I'm not intruding."

Ellie shook her head, motioning for him to come in. "Not at all. We're glad you stopped by."

As Youssef took a seat, his gaze moved between them, studying their expressions. "I heard about your meeting with Professor Malik yesterday. He has been around long enough to know the risks you're facing. I thought you might have questions... or need some advice."

Simon sighed, rubbing his forehead. "He gave us a lot to think about. It's clear that protecting this site means more than just uncovering history. There are people who see artifacts as profit, not as heritage. And Malik believes those people could see us as a threat."

Youssef nodded slowly, his face shadowed by a deep understanding. "Malik is wise, and he's right. Jordan holds treasures beyond measure, but there are those who will go to any length to possess them. These people don't respect history—they see only opportunity."

Ellie's stomach twisted as she thought of Karim's interest in their work. "There's a journalist who visited the site, Karim. He didn't even try to hide his fascination with the artifacts' value. It was... unsettling."

Youssef's face darkened at the mention of Karim's name. "Karim is no mere journalist. He is known in certain circles, and his interest in your dig is likely motivated by something more than academic curiosity. His connections run deep, and he has helped many priceless artifacts vanish into the hands of those who would pay for them."

Ellie's heart pounded. "So you think he's part of this underground network?"

Youssef nodded grimly. "Karim may not be at the center of it, but he is certainly connected. People like him facilitate the sale of history. If he's taken an interest in your site, you can be certain it's because he sees an opportunity."

Simon clenched his fists, his voice calm but resolute. "What do we do, then? We're here to protect this history, but it feels like we're caught in something much larger than we anticipated."

Youssef's gaze softened with understanding. "You're not alone in this. There are people who respect your mission, who see the importance of what you're doing. And I am one of those people. I may not be an archaeologist, but I know the land and the people, and I know how these networks operate."

Ellie felt a surge of gratitude. "Thank you, Youssef. Your support means a lot. But what else can we do to stay safe? We don't want to put ourselves or the dig in jeopardy."

Youssef pulled out a small notebook from his pocket, carefully flipping through the pages. He stopped on a page and handed it to Simon. "This is a contact I trust, a man named Tariq. He has connections throughout Amman and can help keep an eye on things. If Karim or anyone else tries to interfere with your work, Tariq will know."

Simon accepted the paper gratefully, reading the number. "Thank you, Youssef. We'll reach out if anything seems off."

Youssef nodded, his expression grave. "You must also be cautious with what you reveal. The fewer people who know about your findings, the safer you'll be. Artifacts that are left undisturbed are less valuable to people like Karim than those declared priceless."

Ellie sighed, realizing how open they had been about their discoveries. "We hadn't been thinking that way. It's just... we're passionate about what we're finding. We wanted to share it."

Youssef gave a slight smile. "That's understandable, and it's part of the beauty of your work. But discretion can be your greatest asset. If you want to protect this site, sometimes that means sharing less."

He paused, looking out the window at the vast desert beyond. "I have seen what these people are capable of. And if Karim is interested, it's only a matter of time before he begins his schemes. But you're not without allies. Nadia, Malik, even myself—we'll do everything we can to support you."

Ellie's eyes softened. "Thank you, Youssef. We'll take your advice to heart. It's comforting to know we're not alone."

They spoke a while longer, discussing security measures, ways to stay vigilant, and strategies to keep their findings private. Youssef's knowledge of the underground networks and his calm presence reassured them, grounding them in the reality of the risks without stoking their fears.

Finally, Youssef stood, preparing to leave. "Remember what I've told you. And remember that the desert holds many allies. You are here for a reason, and the work you're doing is important."

As he left, Ellie and Simon shared a moment of silence, both of them absorbing the full weight of his words. They knew now that their work was more than just an academic pursuit; it was a mission of protection, a commitment to honoring the past.

After Youssef's departure, Ellie and Simon decided to spend the afternoon at the dig site, taking extra precautions as they cataloged their findings. They worked quietly, their minds sharpened by Malik and Youssef's words, their focus laser-tight on preserving the heritage they'd been entrusted with.

As they examined each artifact, a new level of reverence settled over them. Each piece they unearthed, each symbol they cataloged, was not just a part of history but a piece of a story that had been waiting to be told for centuries. And with Youssef's words fresh in their minds, they understood their role as stewards of this legacy.

Late in the afternoon, Nadia joined them, her presence as calming as ever. She'd sensed a shift in their demeanor and approached them with a supportive smile.

"Youssef came to see you, didn't he?" she asked, her eyes filled with understanding.

Simon nodded. "He did. And his advice was invaluable. He warned us about the risks, but he also reassured us that we have allies. We're grateful to have him—and you—on our side."

Nadia's gaze softened. "Youssef is wise. He's seen the best and the worst that our history brings out in people. And I want you both to know that we're committed to keeping this site safe, no matter what."

Ellie felt a surge of gratitude. "Thank you, Nadia. We're in this together, and that means a lot."

As the sun dipped below the horizon, casting a warm glow over the dig site, Ellie and Simon felt a renewed sense of unity with their team. They weren't just researchers—they were protectors, guardians of a story that belonged to the land and its people.

And as they packed up their tools, ready to return to their apartment, Ellie felt a sense of quiet purpose settle over her. With allies like Youssef, Nadia, and even Tariq, they would face whatever challenges came their way, determined to see this mission through.

When they returned to the apartment that evening, Ellie hung the small talisman from Professor Malik by her bedside, letting its reassuring weight remind her of the promises they'd made to the past and the present. She glanced over at Simon, who gave her a reassuring nod, and knew that together, they were prepared for whatever lay ahead.

But just as she began to relax, a sound broke through the quiet—a faint rustling at their door. She glanced at Simon, who was already sitting up, alert.

Ellie held her breath as they waited, the stillness thick with tension. Someone was out there, someone watching.

And for the first time, Ellie felt a chill of foreboding settle over her. Whatever lay ahead, it was closer than they'd realized.

CLOSE ENCOUNTERS

The next morning arrived in a hazy calm, sunlight casting long shadows across the dig site as Ellie and Simon joined the team. They'd slept fitfully, haunted by the rustling outside their door the night before. It was impossible to ignore the growing sense of being watched, and Professor Malik's and Youssef's warnings weighed heavily on their minds.

As they reached the site, Nadia met them with a look of quiet determination. "After our talk yesterday, I decided to take additional precautions," she said, gesturing toward two new arrivals near the perimeter of the site. The men, clad in plain clothing but with unmistakably vigilant stances, were scanning the area intently. Each one carried a holstered weapon, a detail Nadia didn't seem inclined to mention directly.

"These men are hired security," she continued, her voice low. "They've handled situations like this before. If anyone—even Karim—tries to tamper with the site, they'll ensure he doesn't succeed."

Simon looked from the guards to Nadia, relief mingling with gratitude. "Thank you, Nadia. I think we all feel better knowing they're here."

Nadia gave a small nod. "This site is important. We can't let anything jeopardize it." She paused, her eyes turning steely. "And if Karim shows up again, they'll be ready to handle him."

No sooner had the words left her mouth than a familiar figure appeared in the distance, strolling toward the site with a casual but determined stride. Ellie's heart sank. Karim was back, and this time, he wore an air of confidence that hinted he'd come with a purpose.

Ellie and Simon exchanged a glance, their earlier suspicions flaring to life. But before they could move, Karim closed the distance, a cool smile on his face as he approached.

"Well, well," he said, his voice dripping with mock civility. "I see the Whitcombes are hard at work, uncovering more of the desert's secrets."

Ellie took a steadying breath, determined to stand her ground. "Karim, you've made your interest clear, but we've made ours clear too. This is an archaeological site dedicated to preservation, not to private dealings."

Karim's smile tightened, a flicker of irritation flashing in his eyes. "Ah, but you misunderstand me, Dr. Whitcombe. Preservation is admirable, but let's not pretend that everyone here sees these artifacts as simply relics of the past. Some see... opportunity."

Simon's jaw clenched, his tone turning hard. "We're aware of people who view history that way. But if you're here to suggest we sell or compromise the integrity of our work, you're wasting your time."

Karim's expression darkened, the amiable facade slipping. He took a step closer, lowering his voice. "Let me be clear: I'm not here to make polite suggestions. Artifacts like the ones you've uncovered are worth fortunes to certain buyers, and I'm in a position to make those connections. If you're wise, you'll consider the benefits of cooperation."

Ellie's anger flared, her voice low but unyielding. "This dig is not for sale, Karim. We're here to protect this history, not to pander to buyers."

Karim's smile turned icy, a sinister edge creeping into his gaze. "You're naive if you think your dedication alone will protect you. The people I work with... they don't take kindly to interference. Imagine a setback here—tools go missing, artifacts vanish, or perhaps another 'accidental' cave collapse." His voice dropped to a whisper. "Accidents can happen when amateurs meddle in things they don't understand."

Ellie's mind raced back to the cave collapse, her suspicion crystallizing into certainty. Karim had been involved in that, she was sure of it. And now, he was openly threatening them.

Simon took a step forward, his voice steady but filled with quiet rage. "We're not amateurs, Karim, and we're not alone. You may think you have leverage, but we have support here, people who believe in this dig's purpose. Whatever you're planning, we'll be ready."

Karim's eyes narrowed, a glint of frustration breaking through his smug demeanor. He cast a glance at the security guards who were watching him closely, their hands resting on their holstered weapons, ready to intervene at a moment's notice.

Karim's sneer faded, replaced by a look of calculation. "Ah, so Nadia's resorted to security. Admirable, but hardly a match for what you're up against."

One of the guards took a step closer, his hand firm on his weapon. "Is there a problem here?" he asked, his voice calm but with an underlying authority.

Karim held up his hands in mock surrender, a false smile plastered on his face. "No problem at all. Just a misunderstanding, gentlemen. I'm merely here as an interested observer."

The guard gave a curt nod, his eyes locked on Karim. "Then observe from a distance."

Karim's smile turned bitter, but he backed away, maintaining his faux politeness. "As you wish. But I wouldn't get too comfortable." His gaze lingered on Ellie and Simon, a final, thinly veiled threat in his eyes. "The desert has a way of keeping secrets, after all."

CALLING OF THE ANCIENTS

With that, he turned and walked away, leaving the site under the watchful eyes of the security guards. As soon as he was out of earshot, Ellie let out a shaky breath, her heart still pounding from the confrontation.

Nadia approached them, her face etched with concern. "What did he say to you?"

Ellie swallowed, still shaken. "He... threatened us. Said his associates would interfere with the dig, even cause 'accidents' if we didn't cooperate."

Nadia's eyes narrowed. "Then we'll need to stay vigilant. Karim may be dangerous, but he's also overconfident. He won't realize he's outmatched until it's too late."

Simon looked to the guards, grateful for their presence. "Thank you for bringing in security, Nadia. It's clear Karim is serious about disrupting our work, but at least we know we have a strong defense."

Nadia nodded, her face resolute. "We'll do whatever it takes to protect this site. Karim has connections, but so do we. And as long as you're here, we'll stand with you."

The reassurance strengthened Ellie's resolve, though Karim's threats continued to echo in her mind. She couldn't shake the feeling of being watched, and every shadow seemed to carry the weight of unseen danger. The desert was beautiful, but it held secrets, some of which felt too close for comfort.

As the team returned to their work, the guards maintained a vigilant watch, their presence a constant reminder of the unseen forces hovering just beyond the dig site. Ellie and Simon focused on cataloging the artifacts, taking extra precautions with each new discovery.

Later that evening, as they wrapped up their work and prepared to leave, one of the guards approached them, offering a quick, respectful nod. "We'll be here every day now. Nadia made sure we're prepared for any interference. And if anyone tries to tamper with the site..." He tapped his weapon with a knowing look.

Ellie smiled, a wave of relief washing over her. "Thank you. Knowing you're here makes a world of difference."

The guard gave a small, reassuring smile. "It's our job. We're here to protect, same as you."

As they returned to their apartment that evening, Ellie and Simon felt a mixture of exhaustion and determination. Karim's threats had rattled them, but the presence of the guards and Nadia's unwavering support bolstered their resolve. They were ready for whatever came next.

When they arrived back at the apartment, they found a small note slipped under the door. Ellie picked it up, her brow furrowing as she unfolded the paper. The note was short, but its message was unmistakable:

"You may have allies, but so do I. Be careful what you uncover."

Ellie felt a chill crawl up her spine, the note a reminder that Karim's influence extended far beyond a casual interest in artifacts. She looked up at Simon, her heart pounding with a mix of fear and defiance.

"He's not going to stop," she whispered, her voice barely audible.

Simon took her hand, his grip firm. "Neither are we. If he thinks he can scare us into abandoning this work, he's underestimating just how far we'll go to protect this history."

They spent the rest of the evening formulating their plans, their focus sharper than ever. They would tighten their documentation, increase security around their findings, and keep their allies informed of every move. This dig wasn't just an academic pursuit—it was a mission, one that demanded vigilance and unwavering dedication.

As the hours passed, they read and re-read Professor Malik's notes, reminding themselves of the cultural significance of each artifact and symbol. Karim's threats were nothing compared to the importance of preserving this legacy, and they were determined to honor it.

But as they prepared for bed, Ellie found herself glancing at the talisman hanging by the window, its silent reassurance a comfort in the darkness. She knew that the challenges ahead would test them in ways they hadn't anticipated, but she also knew they were ready.

For they weren't just archaeologists—they were protectors of the past, stewards of a story that demanded to be told.

And no matter what Karim or anyone else tried to throw in their way, they would face it with courage, resilience, and an unshakable belief in the truth of their work.

12

DECIPHERING CLUES

The morning sun had barely risen over Amman when Ellie and Simon made their way to the university to meet with Dr. Khalid Abbas, a renowned historian known for his meticulous work with ancient manuscripts. Khalid was one of the few scholars in the region with access to some of Jordan's rarest documents, including parchment fragments and scrolls passed down through generations.

As they entered the quiet, musty corridors of the university, Ellie felt a renewed sense of excitement mixed with trepidation. Every step felt like it was taking them closer to answers—and, perhaps, deeper into the unknown. She glanced at Simon, whose face mirrored her own anticipation, tempered by caution.

When they reached Dr. Abbas's office, the historian was already waiting for them, seated behind a desk piled with scrolls, maps, and books. He looked up as they entered, his expression warm and welcoming.

"Dr. Whitcombe, Dr. Whitcombe," he greeted, rising to shake their hands. "It's an honor to finally meet you both. I've heard of your work with Dr. al-Masri, and I must say, your findings at the dig site are of great interest to me."

"The honor is ours, Dr. Abbas," Ellie replied, smiling. "We've encountered symbols that seem to defy conventional interpretation, and we're hoping you might be able to shed some light on them."

Dr. Abbas gestured for them to sit, his eyes sparkling with curiosity. "Ah, yes. The language of symbols can be as revealing as it is elusive. Nadia sent me a few of your sketches, and I've reviewed them carefully. They contain certain motifs I've encountered in ancient texts, particularly those describing the rituals of the Nabateans and other, even older, cultures."

Ellie's pulse quickened. "So you recognize them? Are they Nabatean, then?"

Dr. Abbas shook his head slowly, his expression thoughtful. "Not exactly. These symbols are related to the Nabateans but seem to belong to an older lineage, a kind of proto-language that likely predated even the Nabateans. They resemble markings from a forgotten dialect associated with desert tribes—nomads who may have moved through Jordan long before Petra's rise."

Simon leaned forward, intrigued. "So, we're looking at symbols from an ancient culture that has mostly been lost to history?"

"Precisely," Dr. Abbas replied. "Few records exist, but some of the scrolls I've worked with reference a sect known for its rituals and spiritual practices. They viewed the desert as a living entity, a keeper of secrets, and often spoke of temples hidden beneath the sand, believed to be sacred sites for invoking protection."

Ellie felt a thrill run through her as Dr. Abbas continued. The dig site had already felt otherworldly, as if it held stories hidden for millennia. But to hear Dr. Abbas confirm that they might be uncovering a forgotten belief system made the discovery feel all the more powerful.

Dr. Abbas stood, moving over to a bookshelf where he carefully selected a rolled parchment. He returned to the desk, unrolling the fragile scroll with practiced precision, revealing faded symbols etched into the surface.

"These symbols," he said, pointing to a cluster of markings near the top of the scroll, "are similar to some of the ones you discovered. They indicate reverence for something unseen—a force, a guardian of the sands. This deity, or spirit, was believed to protect the desert's secrets, only revealing them to those deemed worthy."

Ellie's gaze flicked between the scroll and Dr. Abbas, her heart pounding. "Do you think we're uncovering one of these sites?"

Dr. Abbas's expression turned solemn. "It's possible. And if that's the case, your work may attract more than just curiosity. Sites like these often carry a certain... mystique, and with it, dangers. Many people, as you've likely already encountered, see such finds as a gateway to wealth. But this culture valued discretion, secrecy. Revealing their mysteries may not sit well with certain individuals or... forces."

Simon exchanged a wary glance with Ellie, his expression filled with concern. "We've already encountered some of that danger. A man named Karim—he's been quite clear about his interest in the artifacts' value."

Dr. Abbas's face darkened. "Karim is well-known. He has ties to individuals who have no respect for history, only profit. You must be careful—his reach is long, and his methods... unsavory."

Ellie felt a chill as Dr. Abbas's words confirmed their worst fears. Karim's influence wasn't limited to idle threats; he was part of a network that would stop at nothing to exploit these finds.

Dr. Abbas seemed to sense their unease and offered a reassuring smile. "But don't lose hope. Your work is important, and you're not alone. I've spoken with Nadia and others who believe in what you're doing. Jordan has many allies for those who seek to protect its heritage."

He pulled another scroll from his collection, this one containing more symbols and a faded map. The map depicted rough sketches of caves and pathways in the desert, marked with symbols similar to those Ellie and Simon had found.

"This map was passed down from a sect of ancient scribes who claimed to have knowledge of hidden temples. If your site aligns with these symbols," Dr. Abbas continued, tracing his finger over the lines, "then you may be standing over something of extraordinary historical value."

Ellie studied the map, captivated. "Could it be a temple site? Or perhaps a sacred meeting place?"

"Possibly," Dr. Abbas replied. "These hidden locations were said to serve as places of worship, gathering, and ritual. But they were fiercely protected, and accessing them was seen as both a privilege and a burden. Those who discovered such sites were expected to guard their secrets."

Simon considered this thoughtfully. "What happened to those who didn't keep the secrets? The ones who tried to reveal what they found?"

Dr. Abbas hesitated, his gaze somber. "They were said to be cursed, plagued by misfortune. The sect believed the desert itself would exact a price for revealing its mysteries. Whether one believes in curses or not, these sites have a history of attracting... unfortunate incidents."

Ellie felt a prickle of unease. They'd already experienced one "unfortunate incident" with the cave collapse, and the threat from Karim loomed over them like a dark cloud. But even as Dr. Abbas spoke of curses, she felt a renewed resolve. They had come here to uncover the truth, and no threat or superstition would stand in their way.

Dr. Abbas leaned back, regarding them with a mixture of respect and concern. "You are brave to continue, given the challenges you face. But remember—the past has a way of protecting itself. If you're careful, respectful, and vigilant, you may find allies even among the desert's mysteries."

Ellie nodded, taking his words to heart. "Thank you, Dr. Abbas. Your insights are invaluable. We'll approach the site with the respect it deserves."

Dr. Abbas smiled, his expression softening. "I have no doubt you will. And please, keep me informed of your findings. The work you're doing is rare, and though it comes with risks, the knowledge you uncover will be priceless."

As they prepared to leave, Dr. Abbas offered them each a small piece of advice. "Trust your instincts. Often, it's intuition that reveals what logic cannot. The desert may be harsh, but it has a way of guiding those who listen."

They left the university with a renewed sense of purpose, Dr. Abbas's words lingering in their minds. The map and symbols offered hints of a larger story, a hidden world that had remained untouched for centuries. They knew now that the site held significance beyond anything they'd imagined.

On the way back, Ellie glanced at Simon, her heart swelling with gratitude for their shared journey. They had faced doubt, danger, and now the possibility of a hidden history that demanded reverence. And yet, they felt closer to the truth than ever.

When they returned to the site that afternoon, they gathered their team and shared Dr. Abbas's insights, showing them the symbols and map. Nadia, Layla, and Amir listened with wide-eyed fascination, their curiosity mingling with a sense of solemnity.

"We're standing over something extraordinary," Nadia murmured, glancing at the dig with a newfound reverence. "We need to be prepared. If this site is as sacred as Dr. Abbas believes, we'll have to work carefully, respectfully, and with utmost caution."

Ellie nodded. "This isn't just another dig. We're protectors, stewards of a story waiting to be told. And we'll treat it with the respect it deserves."

As the team continued their work that day, Ellie and Simon felt a heightened sense of purpose. They weren't simply uncovering artifacts—they were unlocking a forgotten narrative, one that spoke of devotion, sacrifice, and reverence for the land itself.

But as the sun dipped lower in the sky, casting a golden glow over the desert, Ellie couldn't shake the feeling that they were being watched. Karim's threats lingered in her mind, and the thought of curses or "unfortunate incidents" weighed on her more than she cared to admit.

Yet, despite the risks, she felt an unbreakable resolve. They were here to protect the past, to uncover the truths hidden beneath the sands. And no amount of intimidation or superstition would deter them.

As they packed up for the day,

Ellie glanced out at the vast expanse of desert stretching into the horizon. They were bound to this place, linked by a story as old as the sands themselves. And she knew, with a certainty that went beyond words, that they would face whatever challenges lay ahead with courage and resilience.

The desert's secrets were close, almost within reach. And she was ready—whatever the cost—to bring them to light.

CHAPTER 13

A FAMILY CALL

The day's work at the dig site had been intense. Ellie and Simon spent hours analyzing artifacts, comparing the symbols with Dr. Abbas's map, and making notes on each fragment they uncovered. Though each discovery felt like a revelation, Karim's threats and Dr. Abbas's cryptic warnings weighed heavily over them, casting a shadow on their excitement.

As evening settled over their apartment, with darkness creeping through the narrow windows, the familiar chime of Ellie's phone startled them both. She glanced down, surprised to see their youngest son, Nathan, calling. It was unusual for him to reach out on a weekday with the time difference. She knew he must have sensed something off in their recent updates.

"Should we answer it together?" she asked, holding the phone toward Simon. He nodded, recognizing that Nathan would probably want to speak to them both. Ellie swiped to accept the call, propping the phone up so that they both fit within the frame.

The screen flickered for a moment before Nathan's face appeared, his expression a mix of relief and worry. He looked so much like Simon had when they first met—dark, thoughtful eyes and a gaze full of protective concern. Her heart ached with gratitude and a pang of guilt for not sharing more.

"Mom! Dad! It's so good to see you both," Nathan said, though his smile was laced with tension. "I hope I didn't wake you guys."

Ellie gave him a reassuring smile. "Not at all, Nathan. We're glad you called. How are you?"

He sighed, running a hand through his hair, which looked slightly tousled, as if he'd been running his fingers through it for a while. "Better now that I can see you two." He paused, studying their faces. "But, to be honest, I've been worried. I've been talking with Sophie and Oliver, and we all agree—something feels off. You haven't told us much, but we can sense it."

Simon exchanged a quick glance with Ellie, his eyes reflecting a shared regret. They had been keeping things vague in their updates, hoping to avoid causing unnecessary concern. But Nathan's intense gaze made it clear he wasn't going to let them brush off his questions.

"Nathan, I know we haven't told you everything," Simon admitted, leaning closer to the screen. "We didn't want you all to worry too much."

Nathan's expression softened, though his determination remained. "Look, I get it. But we're adults now. We're not kids who need to be shielded. Sophie told me you mentioned something about security, and Oliver thinks someone's trying to interfere with the dig. Are you in danger?"

Ellie hesitated, weighing her words carefully. Nathan, their once-small son who had clung to their tales of adventure, had become a perceptive adult, deeply attuned to their wellbeing. She realized they couldn't hold back the truth any longer.

Taking a deep breath, she began, "Alright, Nathan. We'll be honest with you. This dig has turned out to be... more complex than we originally thought. The artifacts we're uncovering seem to be linked to an ancient culture, maybe even predating the Nabateans. We've found symbols and fragments of a story—something long-hidden in the desert. And because of its historical value, it's attracted the attention of people who... don't care about preservation."

"You mean looters?" Nathan asked, his brows furrowing in alarm.

Simon nodded, his voice steady but serious. "Yes, in a way. There's a man named Karim who's been particularly persistent, even hostile. He's involved with people who would do anything to get their hands on these artifacts, and he's not afraid to use threats to get what he wants."

Nathan's face darkened, his protective instincts flaring. "And you didn't think we'd want to know about this sooner? Mom, Dad, what if something happens to you out there?"

Ellie could see the frustration and worry in Nathan's expression, the desire to protect them even from afar. She felt her own pulse quicken as she tried to choose her words carefully.

"We're doing everything we can to stay safe," she said gently. "We have security at the dig site, and Dr. Nadia al-Masri, who leads the project, has taken extra precautions. We're not alone in this."

"But you're not exactly safe, either," Nathan replied, running a hand over his face. "I mean, this isn't like those hikes or expeditions you used to take us on as kids. This sounds... dark, like there's something dangerous about it."

Simon's gaze softened, and he reached out to the screen as if he could touch Nathan's shoulder. "We're being cautious, son. This is important work, but we're not taking unnecessary risks. Every step we take is careful, and we're surrounded by people who understand the stakes."

Nathan's expression softened, though his worry didn't fade. "I trust you, Dad, but... I feel powerless here. You're halfway across the world, and if something goes wrong, how would we even know?" He paused, visibly struggling to contain his fear. "I just... I'm scared for you both."

Ellie's heart ached as she saw the love and fear in Nathan's face. Nathan had always been the fiercely loyal one, the protector of the family, willing to put everything aside to help his loved ones. But here he was, unable to do anything to keep them safe, and it was clearly eating away at him.

"Believe me, we understand," she said, her voice steady but full of emotion. "But this work feels like something we're meant to do. We've uncovered fragments of a story—a culture that deserves to be remembered. We're careful every day, and we're doing everything we can to protect ourselves and the people working with us."

Nathan nodded slowly, though his face remained solemn. "Just... keep me updated, okay? Not just on the discoveries, but on how you're doing. It's hard to sit here, not knowing if you're safe."

Ellie nodded, reaching out as if she could touch his face through the screen. "We promise, Nathan. We'll keep you in the loop, no matter what."

For a few moments, no one spoke, the quiet filled only by their silent exchange of love and worry. Finally, Nathan broke the silence, managing a small smile. "Just remember, you have a family here who's worried about you. And if anything feels wrong, get out of there."

"We will," Simon said, his voice thick with emotion. "We're proud of you, son. You're wise beyond your years, you know that?"

Nathan smiled, brushing away a stray tear. "Love you both. Promise me you'll be careful."

"We promise," Ellie said softly. "And remember, we're not alone here. We've got people who've lived in Jordan all their lives, people who know the risks and are as dedicated as we are."

As the call ended, Ellie and Simon sat in silence for a few moments, taking in the depth of their conversation. The weight of their children's concern wrapped around them like a protective embrace, mingling with the quiet of the evening. The life they had built, the family they had nurtured, had given them strength and courage they hadn't known they'd needed until this moment.

After a while, Simon reached over, wrapping his arm around Ellie's shoulders, pulling her close. She leaned against him, letting out a soft sigh as he held her.

"You know," he murmured, breaking the silence, "we've shared so many adventures together. And here we are, years later, still drawn to the same path, side by side."

Ellie smiled, lifting her head to meet his gaze. "We're a good team. And if I had to face these risks with anyone, it'd be you."

Simon brushed a strand of hair from her face, his fingers lingering on her cheek. "Then we'll see this through, together. For us. And for them."

He placed a gentle kiss on her forehead, his presence grounding her amidst the swirling concerns. In that moment, the threats, the symbols, the mysteries of the desert seemed distant. What mattered most was the bond they shared—a love that had guided them through decades of adventures and challenges.

As they held each other in the dim light, Ellie felt her resolve harden. They would face whatever came next, both for the sake of history and for the family they would one day return to. Whatever dangers awaited them in the desert, she knew they would face them, together.

With a quiet but renewed sense of purpose, they finally prepared for bed, holding onto the strength of their family's love as they drifted off to sleep.

TEMPLE UNEARTHING

T he air inside the tent was thick with expectation. Even in the cool shade, there was an undercurrent of tension—a sense that something monumental was just beneath the surface, waiting to be uncovered.

Ellie stood over the partially exposed doorway they had been working toward for days. This was the same structure they had initially stumbled upon, the one that had nearly trapped her and Simon in the terrifying cave-in. At the time, they hadn't known what lay beneath them. But after the accident, the entire team had grown more cautious, their efforts becoming slower and more deliberate as they mapped every stone and every symbol. Today, it felt like their patience was about to pay off.

Simon knelt beside her, running his fingers gently over the etched symbols. "These carvings... they seem to echo the ones we saw earlier," he murmured. "But they're more intricate here, as if leading us deeper into the story."

Layla joined them, her eyes bright as she studied the carvings. She'd spent hours reviewing Dr. Abbas's notes and poring over sketches of the symbols they'd previously uncovered. Her excitement was tempered by awe, her voice barely a whisper as she pointed to a pattern carved into the stone above the doorway.

"This symbol here," Layla began, "it's different from the others we've cataloged so far. Dr. Abbas suggested that these might be linked to a guardian deity, but here... the style is older, almost like a precursor. This could be the earliest form of the language, maybe even a ritual language."

Ellie felt her heart quicken. "So, it's possible that this doorway was designed as a threshold. A place meant to keep something in—or perhaps, to keep people out."

Amir, who had been listening quietly, nodded, his gaze fixed on the doorway. "Locals believe the desert guards its own secrets. Some say it's not just sand and stone—it's alive, like a sentient force. Maybe this doorway was a warning, not an invitation."

Simon glanced at Ellie, a flicker of uncertainty in his eyes. "If we're right, then this could be part of a sacred site, protected by rituals lost to time. Whatever lies within, we need to tread carefully."

Just then, one of the workers called out, interrupting the silence. "Dr. Whitcombe! We've cleared the last section."

The team hurried over to see, hearts pounding with anticipation. Beneath the sand lay the unmistakable outline of an ancient doorway, carved with faded symbols that had likely been hidden from the world for centuries. As they brushed away the last remnants of sand, the entrance emerged fully—a portal leading into darkness.

Ellie knelt, her fingers tracing the carvings. "Look at these symbols," she whispered, her voice thick with awe. "These match the markings from Dr. Abbas's scrolls exactly. It's as if we're standing on the threshold of a temple."

Layla's breath caught, her hand reaching out to touch the stone. "This is incredible. Imagine the rituals that took place here, the stories these stones could tell."

The weight of the moment settled over them, a reminder of the responsibility they bore in unearthing these ancient secrets. They weren't just archaeologists anymore—they had become stewards of a history that had waited centuries to be revealed.

Amir took a step back, his gaze filled with both awe and caution. "The desert doesn't give up its secrets easily. If we go further, we need to proceed with respect. There are stories about sites like this—about people who tried to uncover them and were never seen again."

Simon nodded, his expression grave. "We're here to understand and honor, Amir. Nothing more."

They moved together, working with quiet reverence to clear the entrance and brush away the last layers of sand. With every brush stroke, more carvings emerged—figures draped in robes, hands raised in a posture of prayer or supplication. In the center, a towering figure had been carved, shadowy and imposing, as if watching over the temple's threshold.

"This has to be the guardian deity," Ellie murmured. "It's unlike any Nabatean god we've studied before. This figure... it's protective, almost sentinel-like."

Layla studied the figure, her eyes widening with a dawning realization. "Could this be the spirit Dr. Abbas mentioned? The one meant to keep the desert's secrets safe?"

Amir glanced over his shoulder, his expression tense. "If this is a sacred place, then it's unlike anything we've ever seen. It's not just an artifact—it's a remnant of a world we barely understand."

Ellie felt a thrill mixed with trepidation. The initial discovery previously, had hinted at something extraordinary, but she hadn't anticipated just how deeply this excavation would take them into uncharted territory. They were no longer just archaeologists on a dig—they were travelers crossing into a realm of ancient beliefs and spiritual significance.

Simon's voice broke the silence. "Are we ready for this?"

Ellie met his gaze, her voice quiet but certain. "We are here to witness and protect. That's what matters now."

With the entrance fully cleared, they gathered their equipment, preparing to step inside. Layla's hands trembled as she held her flashlight, her excitement tempered by the awareness of the risks they were about to take. Amir's face was set in quiet determination, his reverence for the temple evident with every step.

As they stepped into the temple, the air grew cooler, thick with an ancient, almost reverent silence. Their flashlights illuminated a vast, open space, the walls covered in intricate carvings. Figures bowed in prayer lined the walls, each captured in a moment of worship. The entire room seemed alive with memory, as if the spirits of those who had once worshipped here lingered, watching their every move.

They moved deeper into the sanctuary, documenting the carvings with careful precision. Each wall told a story—a series of rituals, offerings, and prayers etched into stone with painstaking detail. Ellie could feel the weight of the ages pressing down on her, a reminder of the lives that had been devoted to this place.

The realization struck her then, hitting her with a clarity that left her breathless. "Simon," she whispered, her voice urgent. "We need to shield this site immediately."

Simon turned, his face mirroring her concern. "A tent—something to protect the entrance from view and the elements."

They called over the workers, who quickly set about erecting a large, sand-colored canopy over the temple entrance. As they worked, Nadia arrived to oversee the setup, her expression both solemn and proud. She directed the team to add screens around the perimeter for additional privacy.

"We'll need tents and screens around every significant section," Nadia instructed, her voice firm. "Not only for protection from the sun but to ensure that this site remains private. This discovery deserves respect, not prying eyes."

Layla watched as the tent rose, her face a mixture of reverence and relief. "This feels right," she murmured. "This place was hidden for a reason. It deserves to be sheltered."

With the tents and screens in place, the team felt a renewed sense of purpose. Inside the shaded sanctuary, the temple felt even more sacred, shielded from the harshness of the desert outside. It was a small act, but it spoke volumes about their commitment to preserving the legacy they'd uncovered.

Amir walked the perimeter, checking the screens and securing each tent with meticulous care. "It's a sanctuary again," he said quietly. "Now, we can study it with the respect it deserves."

As they finished for the evening, Ellie stood for a moment, gazing at the covered entrance. They had come to Jordan hoping for answers, but they had found so much more—a glimpse into a forgotten world of belief, a world that seemed to be reaching across time to connect with them.

Simon stepped beside her, placing a reassuring hand on her shoulder. "We're part of this story now, Ellie," he said softly. "And we'll protect it, just as its creators intended."

As they made their way back to camp under the dimming light, Ellie knew, deep down, that they had only just begun to scratch the surface. The temple's secrets were close, and she felt a renewed determination to honor the legacy they'd stumbled upon.

For now, though, they would rest, knowing that tomorrow would bring them closer to understanding the ancient echoes hidden beneath the sands.

15

AMBUSHED

The quiet of the desert was almost unnatural as Ellie, Simon, and the team gathered their equipment, ready to return to their accommodations. The excavation had been challenging and exhausting, but each discovery had only deepened their dedication to preserving the temple's story. Still, an unspoken tension filled the air—Karim's threat lingered in Ellie's mind like a shadow. They hadn't seen him since his last confrontation, but she knew he hadn't forgotten them.

They were waiting for Youssef, who'd promised to pick them up at dusk, when the stillness was broken by the low growl of an approaching engine. Simon, always alert, straightened, his gaze hardening as he saw an unfamiliar dark SUV speeding toward them, kicking up a cloud of dust.

"That's not Youssef," Ellie murmured, a feeling of dread settling in her stomach.

The SUV skidded to a stop just yards away, and Karim stepped out, flanked by two men whose expressions were anything but friendly. Karim's eyes settled on Ellie and Simon, a thin, unsettling smile stretching across his face. His associates moved to his sides, hands resting in a way that suggested they were ready for a confrontation.

"Dr. Whitcombe," Karim greeted, his voice smooth and mocking. "Still here, despite my friendly advice? I would have thought by now you'd see the wisdom in leaving."

Simon stepped protectively in front of Ellie, his jaw clenched. "We're here for an official dig, Karim. We're not interested in anything you're doing here."

Karim's smile faded, his eyes glinting with malice. "You're interfering with matters you don't understand. I'm here to give you a final warning—leave, or face the consequences."

Ellie's pulse quickened as she noticed one of Karim's men reaching into his jacket, the unmistakable glint of a weapon catching the last rays of the sun. She squeezed Simon's hand, her own hands growing clammy with fear.

Just then, the rumble of another engine filled the air, and Youssef's car appeared, speeding toward them. Relief washed over Ellie as Youssef's car came to a halt, and he stepped out, his posture calm but watchful as he assessed the situation.

"Is there a problem here?" Youssef asked, his tone steady and unbothered.

Karim's gaze flickered over Youssef with irritation. "Nothing that concerns you, driver. I suggest you turn around and mind your business."

Youssef's eyes narrowed slightly, but he didn't move. "I'm here to take Dr. Whitcombe and her team back safely. That's my business."

Karim's calm facade cracked, anger flaring in his eyes. "You don't understand who you're dealing with, Youssef. These people aren't worth the trouble."

Youssef held his ground, his gaze unwavering. "I'll be the judge of that."

With a dismissive wave, Karim turned back to Ellie and Simon, his voice low and venomous. "Last chance, Dr. Whitcombe. Leave, or I promise you'll regret it."

Ignoring Karim's threat, Youssef gestured for Ellie and the team to get into his car. "Now," he urged, urgency in his voice. They climbed in quickly, closing the doors as Youssef hit the gas.

As they sped away, Ellie glanced back and saw Karim and his men scrambling into their SUV. A chill ran down her spine as she realized they weren't giving up. The head-lights of the dark SUV grew brighter, closing the distance with every second.

"They're following us!" Layla cried, clutching the back of the seat in fear.

Youssef kept his gaze steady, his voice calm but intense. "Hold on. They may know this desert, but I know it better."

He veered sharply off the main track, steering the car over rough, uneven ground that bounced them against their seats. Ellie clung to the handle above the door as they hurtled over rocks and through clouds of sand. In the rearview mirror, she saw the SUV trailing closely, Karim's grim expression visible through the dust.

Simon leaned forward, his face pale. "Can we lose them in the dunes?"

Youssef's eyes flashed with determination. "I'll try. Stay low!"

He swerved into a narrow pass flanked by towering dunes, guiding the car through a winding path. But Karim's SUV kept pace, bouncing over the dunes, headlights bouncing wildly. Ellie's heart hammered as they jolted over a steep incline, sand spraying up around them.

Suddenly, a loud crack split the air. A bullet had struck the sand beside them, sending up a spray of dust.

"They're shooting at us!" Ellie's voice was tight with fear as she ducked down, pulling Simon with her.

Youssef tightened his grip on the wheel. "Stay down. I'll get us out of here."

He sped through the dunes, weaving between sand banks and taking sharp turns to throw off Karim's aim. Another gunshot rang out, and this time, the bullet grazed the rear of the car, leaving a jagged dent in the metal. Ellie held her breath, every muscle tense as Youssef pushed the car to its limits.

Just when it seemed they had lost them, the SUV reappeared, barreling down a dune, its headlights bearing down on them like twin predators. Karim's men leaned out of the windows, their guns aimed steadily at Youssef's car.

Youssef swerved suddenly, steering them toward a rocky outcrop and narrowly missing another bullet. "Hang on," he warned, his voice fierce with concentration.

They lurched up a steep incline, the rocky terrain jolting them violently, and Ellie heard the sharp crack of gunfire echoing off the rocks. She clung to the seat, feeling Simon's hand grip hers tightly as they clambered over the rough terrain.

Finally, they crested the hill, and Youssef braked sharply, switching off the lights and pulling behind a towering boulder. He gestured for silence, and they all held their breath as Karim's SUV sped past, its lights sweeping over the valley below.

They waited in tense silence, listening to the roar of Karim's engine fade into the distance. After several agonizing minutes, Youssef exhaled slowly, his grip on the wheel relaxing.

"They've gone," he murmured. "But we're not out of danger yet. Karim won't give up."

"We can't go back to the apartment," Simon said, his voice steady but tense. "It's too risky. They'll expect us to return there."

Ellie nodded, her mind racing. "Nadia needs to know what happened. We'll need backup if we're going to continue the excavation."

Youssef pulled out his phone, dialing Nadia's number. She picked up on the first ring, her voice sharp with concern. Ellie could only hear one side of the conversation, but

Youssef's explanation was quick and tense. When he hung up, he turned back to them, his expression resolute.

"Nadia's arranging the security team and herself to reconvene to a safe location. We'll be meeting them in the morning," he explained, glancing at the others. "For now, we're going somewhere safe for the night. It's an old friend's house in the outskirts of Amman—Karim won't think to look there."

They navigated carefully, staying off the main roads and using only their parking lights to avoid drawing attention. The desert stretched out around them, a vast and shadowed expanse, as they drove in tense silence.

After nearly an hour of careful maneuvering, they arrived at a small, isolated compound nestled among tall date palms. The house looked weathered but solid, with a tall gate that Youssef unlocked with a quick motion. He drove them inside, parking the car in a covered garage out of sight.

"We'll be safe here," he assured them, guiding them into the house. The interior was modest but welcoming, with a few scattered rugs and a faint scent of incense. Youssef's friend, an elderly man named Rafiq, greeted them with warm hospitality despite the late hour.

Ellie, still shaken from the chase, took a seat on one of the low couches, feeling the adrenaline slowly drain from her system. Simon sat beside her, wrapping an arm around her shoulders as she leaned into him.

Rafiq brought out tea and water, placing the tray on the low table in front of them. "Youssef tells me you've had a difficult night," he said kindly. "My home is yours for as long as you need."

"Thank you, Rafiq," Ellie replied, her voice thick with gratitude. "Your hospitality means more than you know."

Youssef stayed near the window, his gaze scanning the horizon as if expecting Karim to appear at any moment. He turned to the group, his voice serious. "Karim won't give up easily. We'll need to stay here until Nadia's team arrives. Tomorrow, we can plan the next steps."

***

The quiet of Rafiq's house was a stark contrast to the roaring chase they'd just escaped. Shadows flickered on the walls from an old oil lamp that Rafiq had placed in the center of the room, casting a soft, comforting glow. Ellie took a long sip of tea, her hands still shaking slightly as she cradled the warm cup.

"Ellie, Simon," Youssef said quietly, taking a seat across from them. "I know tonight's events were frightening. But you should understand—Karim is not just a man after antiquities. He's deeply entrenched in the black market trade, and his clients include some very dangerous people. They will stop at nothing."

Simon nodded, his face drawn with worry. "We knew this project would be challenging, but we didn't anticipate... this level of threat."

Youssef leaned forward, his gaze serious. "Karim sees this temple as an opportunity. But for him, it's not about preservation or history—it's about profit and power. The artifacts you've uncovered, especially the ones tied to ritual, are highly sought after. And he's not the type to back down easily."

Layla, who had been sitting quietly beside Amir, looked up, her eyes wide with fear. "So what do we do now? We can't just abandon the site... can we?"

Ellie shook her head, her voice calm but resolute. "No, we can't. We're here to protect the history we've uncovered, and that hasn't changed. But we need to be smart about this. Karim has escalated things, so we need to respond in kind."

Youssef nodded approvingly. "I'll speak with Nadia in the morning to arrange for additional security measures. Until then, it's best to stay here. Rafiq's house is far enough away that Karim won't think to look for you here."

Rafiq, who had been observing quietly, offered them a warm smile. "You are safe here. The desert watches over those who respect it. And I will do everything in my power to keep you protected."

As the conversation continued, a deep exhaustion began to settle over the group. They each found makeshift places to rest within the modest sanctuary of Rafiq's home, though sleep remained elusive. Ellie lay beside Simon on a small mat, listening to the quiet murmur of Youssef and Rafiq's voices as they stood watch by the window.

"I can't believe how quickly things have escalated," Simon whispered, his arm around Ellie as he stared up at the ceiling. "One day, we're excited about the dig, and now... we're hiding from gunfire."

Ellie turned to look at him, a sad smile playing on her lips. "We knew archaeology wasn't always glamorous, but I don't think either of us expected this. Yet, I can't shake the feeling that we're meant to see this through. It's as if the temple is calling to us, and somehow, protecting it has become our purpose."

Simon nodded, tightening his hold on her. "Then we'll face it together. No matter what, we'll keep each other safe."

Eventually, exhaustion overtook them, and they drifted into a restless sleep, haunted by the images of flashing headlights and the echo of gunshots.

Morning arrived in a blaze of desert sunlight, streaming through the narrow windows of Rafiq's home. Ellie blinked awake, disoriented for a moment, before the memory of the previous night's events came rushing back. She sat up, rubbing her eyes, and saw that Youssef and Rafiq were already preparing tea and bread for breakfast.

"Good morning," Youssef greeted, his face serious but warm. "Nadia called a few minutes ago. She's arranged for additional security, and her team is on their way here to discuss the situation. We'll make a plan for the next few days."

Ellie nodded, her expression resolute. "Thank you, Youssef. For everything. I don't know how we would have managed without you."

Youssef offered her a small smile. "It's my duty, Dr. Whitcombe. I believe in what you're doing, and I'll see it through with you."

As the others stirred awake, Rafiq served the breakfast, his calm presence a reassuring force amid the tension. Shortly after, they heard the hum of an approaching vehicle, and Nadia's car pulled up outside, followed by two more vehicles with a small team of security personnel. Nadia stepped out, her face set with determination, and greeted Ellie and Simon with a reassuring hug. Alongside her, was Amir, who shook their hands profusely, thanking God they were safe.

"I'm so sorry about last night," Nadia said, her voice low. "I'm glad you're all safe. Karim is a dangerous man, but we're not going to let him drive you out. The history here is too important."

Ellie nodded, her voice steady. "Thank you for bringing in additional security. I think we'll need every measure we can get."

Nadia passed to Ellie a bag containing extra clothes, toiletries and the like, for their sudden stay at Rafiq's home.

They gathered in the main room to discuss their strategy, a large map of the desert laid out on the table. The security team, led by a man named Omar, explained that they would set up a perimeter around the site, with regular patrols to ensure no one approached unnoticed.

"We'll also have guards stationed near the tents themselves," Omar continued, his voice calm and professional. "If Karim or his men come near the site again, they won't get close enough to cause trouble."

Layla and Amir exchanged relieved looks, though their faces remained tense with worry. The additional security was reassuring, but Ellie knew that the presence of guards would only escalate Karim's determination to get his hands on the artifacts.

After laying out the security plans, Nadia turned to the team. "I know last night was difficult, but if you're willing, I'd like you to return to the site this afternoon. The sooner we get back to work, the sooner we can secure and document everything properly."

Ellie looked at Simon, who gave her a small nod of encouragement. They couldn't let Karim's threats keep them away. If anything, the events of the previous night had only strengthened their resolve.

"We're ready," Ellie replied, her voice firm. "Let's finish what we started."

That afternoon, with the new security team in place, they returned to the site. Armed guards stood watch near the perimeter, their eyes scanning the desert for any signs of movement. Omar coordinated the patrols, ensuring that every angle was covered. As Ellie entered the tented structure that housed the temple entrance, she felt a renewed sense of purpose.

The day passed in focused silence, each member of the team moving carefully, as if the events of the previous night had infused them all with a heightened awareness of their surroundings. Layla and Amir worked beside Ellie, their faces drawn with concentration as they cataloged carvings and artifacts.

By evening, they had made significant progress, and Ellie felt a deep sense of satisfaction despite the lingering tension in the air. As they packed up for the day, she caught Simon's gaze, and he gave her an encouraging smile.

"We're doing it," he said quietly, his voice filled with pride. "No matter what, we're honoring this history."

Just as they were about to leave, one of the guards approached, his expression tense. "Dr. Whitcombe, we spotted a vehicle a few miles out. It's stationary, but we're monitoring it closely."

Ellie's heart skipped a beat, but she forced herself to stay calm. "Thank you. Keep us updated, and let me know if it moves closer."

The team moved quickly to gather their things, and under the watchful eyes of the guards, they climbed into Youssef's car. As they drove back to Rafiq's house, Ellie couldn't shake the feeling that Karim was watching, waiting for his next opportunity. She knew he wouldn't stop until he got what he wanted.

Later that evening, they sat together around a small fire in Rafiq's courtyard, the soft crackling of flames a welcome contrast to the noise and chaos of the past two days. Rafiq's hospitality continued to be a balm to their weary spirits, and the quiet camaraderie of the team brought a sense of normalcy back to the group.

Simon turned to Ellie, his expression thoughtful. "Do you think it's worth it?" he asked, his voice barely above a whisper.

Ellie paused, considering his question. She thought of the ancient carvings, the stories embedded in the walls, the silent testimony of those who had once worshipped within the temple. "Yes," she said softly. "History doesn't belong to people like Karim. It belongs to all of us, and I think... I think we have a responsibility to protect it."

Simon nodded, taking her hand in his. "Then we'll see it through. No matter what."

As the fire crackled and embers drifted into the night, Ellie's resolve grew stronger. She looked around at the faces of her team, each of them bound by a shared commitment that transcended personal safety. Whatever challenges lay ahead, they would face them together, united by the belief that history's legacy was worth defending, no matter the cost.

JOURNEYING TO THE PAST

Ellie's footsteps echoed faintly as she stepped into the temple's cool depths, her heart racing with anticipation. Even the air felt thick with history, as if the secrets of ancient worlds were waiting just beneath the surface, ready to be unveiled. Her flashlight cast a narrow beam along the passage, illuminating intricate carvings that danced and shifted under the glow, whispering stories from ages past.

Nadia was close behind her, carrying a tablet and camera to document each new discovery. Her face, usually composed and focused, was alive with excitement. She motioned for Ellie to slow down, her gaze fixed on a series of carvings along the walls. "Look here," she murmured, voice filled with reverence as she traced her finger over a series of symbols. "These inscriptions are far older than any others we've found in the area. This site might have been dedicated to a deity or spirit beyond what we know, possibly one even older than Nabatean traditions."

Simon, joining them with Layla and Amir, moved his flashlight along the passage's edge. "It's amazing how well-preserved this is," he said, his voice low. "It feels like they meant for us to find it exactly like this—as if it's frozen in time, waiting."

Nadia nodded, her fingers still following the lines carved into the stone. The figure before them was cloaked and faceless, with outstretched arms, flanked by symbols of animals, plants, and small flame-like markings. "This is what some ancient tribes called a 'realm guardian,'" she explained. "The desert tribes believed in spirits or deities who watched over not just specific places but whole ecosystems. But this... there's something even more powerful about this one."

Ellie studied the figure closely. Unlike other depictions of deities, this guardian had a fluid shape, like it was part of the elements, melding into the symbols around it. "It's as if it's not just one element, but the whole desert itself," she said.

Dr. Abbas's theories about a deity that lived within the desert's sands, wind, and heat flashed through Ellie's mind. "The symbols we found in the cave—maybe they were an offering, something to gain favor from this guardian spirit."

Layla tilted her head, her brow furrowed as she examined a set of faint symbols on the opposite wall. "This isn't like any other script we've seen in Jordan. It's almost as if it predates the other forms, as if this was the first language, something meant for ritual or sacred purposes only."

Nadia glanced at her, eyes glinting with excitement. "You're absolutely right. Ancient temples often contained scripts or images meant to be read by the initiated alone. Some believe they used special symbols to communicate directly with their gods or the spirits of the dead."

As they moved deeper, they noticed the walls were lined with small, carefully carved niches. Inside each niche sat a different artifact—a piece of pottery, a tiny, elegant figurine, a metal implement that glinted in the flashlight's beam. The quiet stillness of these ancient objects felt reverent, and Ellie found herself wondering about the hands that had placed them here centuries before.

"These artifacts," Nadia said, breaking the silence, "they were likely used in the rituals depicted on the murals. Each of them had a purpose. Some may have represented elements, others might have been offerings." She picked up a small clay tablet, its surface covered in looping symbols. "This tablet is an incredible find. I haven't seen anything quite like this script before—it looks proto-Arabic, perhaps a precursor to what we know."

Amir cleared his throat, his voice laced with awe. "This place feels... alive, almost as if it's aware of us. It's not like any other temple I've been in. There's reverence here, but something else... intensity."

Nadia turned to him, her face serious. "You're not wrong. In many ancient cultures, temples weren't just places to pray. They were gateways between worlds, places where the divine met the mortal. This temple might have served as a passage for souls, a place to guide them from this world to the next."

A chill ran down Ellie's spine, but it wasn't unpleasant. She felt as though she'd been drawn into the heart of something ancient and mysterious, a story that demanded to be told.

They rounded a corner, and suddenly, their flashlights illuminated an enormous mural stretching across the wall. Ellie's breath caught. The mural depicted a series of ceremonies, each one filled with masked figures engaged in strange, rhythmic dances, offering gestures, and presenting gifts. Every figure wore elaborate costumes, masks decorated with feathers, beads, and fragments of bone. In the background, a large, shadowy form loomed—a figure whose presence seemed to grow in each scene, more defined and dominant as the story unfolded.

"This is like a narrative," Layla said, stepping closer to the wall. "Every image is part of a ritual, almost like we're looking at frames from an ancient movie."

Nadia's voice was soft with awe. "This isn't just a deity. It's a god of life and death. See how it watches over every ceremony, present in every scene as a guardian of the cycle."

Simon's flashlight traced the outlines of the dark figure, his expression troubled. "It's almost like they're preparing for something. Maybe it was a transformation or some kind of journey."

"Yes," Nadia murmured, her gaze faraway. "In ancient times, transformation was one of the highest rituals. Death wasn't seen as an end, but as a passage. This temple may have been a place to prepare the soul, to honor the mystery of crossing from one world to another."

As Ellie studied the mural, she felt a strange sense of movement in the scenes. It was as though she could hear the beat of drums, the low hum of voices chanting across centuries. The figures seemed alive, replaying their sacred rites, reliving their journey through each painted line and detail.

One section of the mural depicted figures offering small stones, their hands extended as though the stones held a divine energy. Ellie felt her pulse quicken—these stones looked almost identical to the ones they had uncovered in the cave, nestled beside the symbols they'd first found.

"These stones," she murmured, pointing to the mural, "are similar to the ones we found in the earlier dig. This mural might be a guide, showing us how they connected with their god."

Nadia's eyes lit up as she examined the stones. "If these stones were conduits, a way to reach this guardian deity, it's likely they held symbolic or spiritual energy. This temple isn't just an ancient monument. It's a living place, a site where rituals could still hold power."

Amir glanced at her, his face solemn. "If Karim's men get wind of these objects, they'll strip everything away. They won't respect what it means."

Simon placed a firm hand on Ellie's shoulder, his gaze serious. "That's why we're here, Ellie. We'll make sure this history is honored and protected."

They moved further down the mural, where they discovered a small, rounded chamber. In the center sat an altar, adorned with fragments of cloth, dried plants, and small statues placed carefully around its edge. Ellie knelt in front of the altar, feeling a deep sense of humility as she examined the objects. Each item, worn and fragile, carried the weight of centuries.

"Altars were often the heart of temples," Nadia explained. "Here, people could bring their wishes, their fears, and their hopes, channeling it all to the deity. This altar has seen countless ceremonies, countless voices raised in prayer."

Ellie looked at her, a question burning in her mind. "Nadia, do you think this temple's power could still exist? If people truly believed in these rituals... is it possible that their devotion lingers here?"

Nadia's expression softened, and she gave a slow nod. "Belief is powerful, Ellie. It's not bound by time. I believe this temple holds the energy of everyone who has ever stood here, who has ever prayed, and perhaps even those who will one day follow."

The team fell silent, feeling the immense weight of the temple's presence. This wasn't just an excavation. They were entering a story that spanned generations, stretching from the ancient past into the present.

After documenting the altar and its relics, they began to make their way back. Each step they took out of the temple felt like peeling back from a sacred moment, each artifact they left behind a reminder of the reverence the space demanded. As they reached the entrance, Ellie turned to take one last look at the temple's silent, shadowed halls.

The desert stretched endlessly before them, vast and unknowable. Ellie felt a sense of peace settle over her as she looked back at the temple, knowing they'd honored its history and its secrets.

Nadia stepped beside her, her gaze steady. "We're part of this place's story now. Whatever happens next, we have a duty to protect it."

Ellie nodded, her mind brimming with the artifacts and stories they'd uncovered. Karim's threats and their close encounter in the desert still lingered, but her purpose felt clear. Whatever it took, they would stand as guardians of this ancient world, preserving its legacy for those yet to come.

The team shared a silent vow, bound by their commitment to history and to one another. The ancient world had chosen them to uncover its secrets—and they wouldn't let it down.

***

As the sun dipped below the horizon, casting the desert in hues of orange and purple, the team returned to Rafiq's house. They had left the temple reluctantly, each of them feeling as though the stones themselves were bidding them to stay. Ellie couldn't shake the feeling that they had barely scratched the surface of what lay within.

Back at the safe house, they gathered around a small fire Rafiq had prepared in the courtyard, the air thick with the scents of spices and herbs he'd burned to "ward off unwanted eyes," as he put it. Despite the warmth of the flames, Ellie pulled her shawl closer. The evening had a chill that felt different, a weight that pressed upon them like a shadow from the ancient past.

Nadia held a small notebook in her hands, flipping through her hastily scrawled notes. "The more I think about it," she began, her voice barely louder than a whisper, "the more I believe this site is connected to a legend I once read—a guardian spirit believed to be embedded within the desert itself. The Bedouin called it *al-Hafiz*, 'the Watcher,' a protector that would reveal itself to those with pure intentions."

Layla leaned forward, her eyes wide with awe. "You think the temple might be... its domain? That it's more than a place of worship, but something it guards, or even inhabits?"

Nadia nodded. "Yes. And every part of it—the altar, the mural, even the stones—serves as a conduit to connect worshipers directly to this presence. It was a way to honor *al-Hafiz*, to remain in its favor."

Ellie glanced over at Simon, her heart pounding. "If this Watcher is truly part of the desert, then it's possible the spirit still lingers, watching over the temple and everything connected to it. And if that's true, Karim and his men are in more danger than they realize."

Simon rubbed his chin thoughtfully. "If there's even a chance that the guardian's spirit is still alive within that temple, it might explain why we've felt so... drawn to it. And why the cave collapse felt like more than just a natural accident."

"Exactly," Nadia agreed, her eyes gleaming with excitement. "This is no ordinary excavation. We're not simply uncovering relics; we're engaging with a legacy that spans millennia. This temple was meant to be protected by those who understood its power and significance."

Rafiq listened quietly, his face thoughtful. When they paused, he spoke up, his voice low and steady. "The desert keeps secrets for a reason. The tribes have long known that it holds both blessings and curses. If this Watcher exists, it has allowed you into its sanctuary—but it may not be so welcoming to Karim."

Ellie considered this, a thought forming in the back of her mind. "So if we're to protect the temple, maybe we need to honor it ourselves. Perhaps there's something we can do to align ourselves with its spirit, to guard it from those who only want to exploit it."

Nadia leaned forward, intrigued. "You're suggesting we perform some kind of protective ritual, to show that our intentions are pure?"

Simon frowned, his gaze uncertain. "Are we really prepared for that? We're scientists, not practitioners of ancient magic. There's so much we don't understand about this temple or what it represents."

Ellie looked at him, determination sparking in her eyes. "I don't think we need to understand everything—only to show respect, to acknowledge the spirit that guards this place. This may be the only way to truly safeguard the temple from Karim. If we don't, everything we've uncovered could be lost or desecrated."

The team fell into contemplative silence, each of them weighing the gravity of Ellie's words. Layla looked between them, her face alight with resolve. "Then let's do it. We're already bound to this place in a way none of us could have anticipated. If we must perform a ritual to honor it, then I'm willing."

Nadia nodded, her face thoughtful. "I'll research some traditional rituals associated with the desert. There may be symbols, words, or gestures we can replicate to channel our intentions. But we'll have to be cautious. Rituals can be powerful, and if we perform it poorly, it could bring unintended consequences."

Amir looked uneasy, but he finally nodded. "I'll help too. I know some people who might have insights into ancient rites from this region. If we're serious about this, we'll need all the guidance we can get."

As they discussed plans for the ritual, Ellie noticed that Youssef was standing near the courtyard's edge, his eyes fixed on the dark desert beyond the safe house walls. She approached him quietly, sensing his unease.

"Youssef, are you all right?" she asked softly.

He turned to her, his expression serious. "Ellie, I trust in what you're doing, but I also feel... something is out there, watching. I don't know if it's Karim's men or something else. But tonight, I'll stay on guard. You need to focus on your work without fear."

Ellie touched his arm in gratitude, feeling a wave of reassurance. "Thank you, Youssef. You've been a loyal friend to us all."

Youssef nodded, his expression somber. "If there is a guardian spirit in that temple, then perhaps it will protect us as we honor it. But be careful. Ancient beings, if they exist, can be unpredictable. This is sacred ground we're dealing with."

Ellie returned to the others, feeling a renewed sense of resolve. They had a mission, one far greater than themselves, and for the first time, she sensed that perhaps the desert had chosen them to protect its secrets.

As the hours passed, they gathered supplies and prepared mentally for the ritual that would take place at dawn. Nadia carefully transcribed an ancient chant she remembered from a text she'd read years ago, and Layla gathered small offerings of dried herbs, stones, and desert flowers to leave at the altar.

When dawn's first light streaked across the horizon, they traveled back to the temple, moving in quiet procession through the cool sands. The atmosphere around them felt charged, as if the desert itself were holding its breath, waiting to see what they would do.

Inside the temple, they lit a small fire at the altar, arranging the offerings carefully. Nadia led the ritual, her voice steady as she recited the words she'd translated, a soft, rhythmic chant that seemed to fill the chamber with an otherworldly hum. The sound reverberated off the walls, echoing through the ancient stone, as if the spirit of the temple itself were stirring in response.

Each of them took a turn placing an offering on the altar, bowing their heads in silence. When it was Ellie's turn, she closed her eyes, feeling a rush of emotions as she set her offering—a small, polished stone from her travels—on the altar.

"I ask for your protection," she murmured, her voice filled with quiet reverence. "We are here to honor you, to keep your story alive. We ask that you guard us, as we promise to guard you."

A strange silence followed, settling over the temple like a thick fog. Ellie felt an almost tangible energy fill the air, a sense of presence that seemed to acknowledge their words, their intentions.

They left the temple quietly, each of them feeling a profound sense of peace as they emerged into the morning sunlight. Simon walked beside Ellie, his expression one of wonder and disbelief.

"Did you feel that?" he whispered. "It was as if the temple... responded."

Ellie nodded, her heart full. "I think we did what we needed to do. Now, we have to trust that the guardian spirit will do its part."

As they made their way back to the safe house, Ellie cast one last look at the temple in the distance, feeling the silent power of its presence. She knew the journey ahead would be fraught with challenges, but she no longer felt alone. They were bound to the temple's legacy, its ancient spirit guiding them every step of the way.

17

KARIM STRIKES

The quiet inside Rafiq's safe house felt almost oppressive as the team gathered around the low table, discussing the day's discoveries. Their thoughts lingered on the temple and the significance of the mural, each member feeling the weight of their mission to protect and preserve the ancient site. Ellie sat close to Simon, taking comfort in the steady presence of his hand over hers. The ritual they'd performed still lingered in her mind, a reassuring memory amid the dangers surrounding them.

But as night deepened, a heavy knock shattered the calm. The door creaked open to reveal one of the guards assigned by Nadia's contacts at the Ministry. His expression was somber, worry lining his face.

"There's been a break-in at the site," he said quietly.

A shocked silence followed his words, and Ellie felt her heart sink. She exchanged a tense look with Simon. They'd taken every precaution—employing trusted security guards, taking only duplicates of their research to the dig, and leaving primary records and artifacts safely stored at Rafiq's house. But Karim's persistence was clear: he would exploit any vulnerability.

Without delay, they gathered what they needed and followed the guard into the cooling desert night. The ride back to the site felt longer than usual, every bump in the road heightening Ellie's anxiety. Karim's reach was daunting, but it was the ruthlessness of this move—invading a historic site—that made her stomach churn.

When they arrived, Ellie took in the damage with a sinking heart. Several tents lay torn and trampled, their contents scattered across the sand. The makeshift barriers, usually secure and organized, were now disarrayed, and a guard who'd been on night duty described finding key areas compromised, as though the intruders had specifically targeted places where notes and documentation were kept.

Nadia's eyes narrowed as she surveyed the damage. "They knew exactly where to strike," she said. "This wasn't a random break-in. Whoever came had a purpose, and it wasn't just vandalism."

Layla knelt beside a pile of torn pages, sifting through what remained of their field sketches. Her face tightened with emotion as she inspected Ellie's delicate, now crumpled, sketches of the carvings they'd just finished cataloging the day before.

Ellie felt a fierce anger flare within her. They'd taken precautions, leaving only secondary notes onsite and carefully storing artifacts and primary records offsite each night. Yet Karim had made his message clear—he wasn't just after artifacts; he wanted to make them feel vulnerable and threatened.

Then Simon, moving around the remains of a toppled equipment box, spotted a large piece of paper pinned to one of the tent poles, flapping in the night breeze. When he peeled it free, Ellie felt a chill run down her spine. It was one of their maps, defaced in thick red ink. A single word stretched across it: *Leave.*

"This is personal," Ellie murmured, voice low but steady. Karim had moved from shadowed threats to outright intimidation, and he clearly wanted them gone.

Simon's expression hardened as he looked around at the wreckage. "Then he's underestimating us. We've come too far to abandon this now."

Nadia's face was tense but resolved. "But we can't ignore this. Karim's crossed a serious line. This is a protected site, and he's disregarded every rule to send his message. We need the Ministry's help now more than ever."

Youssef, who had been watching the perimeter quietly, approached. "The Ministry's support will give us leverage, but Karim has connections. If we escalate, we'll need patience. He won't go down easily."

Nadia nodded, already pulling out her phone. "I'll reach out to my contacts within the Ministry immediately. They need to know the extent of this break-in. If they intervene, we'll have the leverage to pressure the police to take action."

Ellie felt a surge of relief, mixed with a flicker of hope. The Ministry of Antiquities had influence that could bolster their defenses, something beyond what local law enforcement alone could offer. Karim might be relentless, but she was confident that this pushback could send him a stronger message.

The team spent the next few hours salvaging anything of value and carefully gathering what could still be saved. The guards had found that the intruders had deliberately avoided areas with less relevance to their research, instead focusing on damaging or defacing documents that had only recently been created. Ellie, with Layla beside her, worked through the remaining sketches and notes, marking what could be copied or redone. Despite the mess, she was grateful that their primary artifacts and notes were safely secured at Rafiq's house, untouched by Karim's men.

Layla's voice trembled as she sifted through damaged papers. "I can't believe anyone would go this far just to send a warning. It's... senseless."

Ellie placed a hand on her arm. "Karim doesn't see history the way we do. For him, it's something to control and exploit. But our work isn't about control—it's about giving history its due, allowing these stories to exist. That's why we can't let him win."

As the first light of dawn broke, they returned to Rafiq's house with what remained, setting up a temporary workspace in one of the spare rooms. Nadia made several phone calls, her words carefully chosen as she described the situation to her Ministry contacts. Ellie, exhausted but fueled by determination, began recreating sketches and notes with Simon's help, rebuilding from memory what they had lost.

A few hours later, Nadia gathered them all in the main room, her face resolute as she relayed the Ministry's response.

"The Ministry's sending officials to assess the damage and reinforce security measures around the site," she announced. "They'll handle the investigation and have authorized us to bring in local police for backup. We'll be getting the support we need."

A sense of relief swept over them. Ellie knew this wouldn't stop Karim outright, but the Ministry's involvement changed the dynamics. It brought a new layer of protection, one that Karim would have difficulty bypassing.

Amir, arms crossed, voiced the question on everyone's mind. "Do you think the police will actually take this seriously?"

Nadia nodded, her tone firm. "With the Ministry pushing for action, they'll have no choice. But we need to be vigilant. We can't rely solely on outside help."

Youssef stepped forward, his expression focused. "I know a few locals who can act as additional eyes. They know the desert well and can recognize unusual activity. With a little pay, they'll be loyal to our cause."

Ellie glanced at him, gratitude clear in her eyes. "Thank you, Youssef. We'll need all the support we can get. Karim's persistence is unlike anything I've encountered."

They solidified their security plans, organizing shifts to monitor the site and arranging regular check-ins with the Ministry officials. Rafiq offered to host them as long as they needed, insisting that his home would remain a safe haven for those honoring history.

That afternoon, the Ministry officials arrived—a small team led by a dignified man named Ahmed, whose calm authority brought a sense of stability to the situation. He listened carefully as Nadia detailed the break-in, assessing the damage with a steady gaze.

After inspecting the site, Ahmed turned to the group, his tone grim. "This incident is a serious violation, both legally and culturally. I'll arrange for additional security and push for police involvement. We're seeing more interference from black-market networks, but this situation demands immediate intervention."

Ellie felt a renewed confidence as Ahmed outlined the Ministry's next steps. Karim might have local power, but this level of attention from the Ministry would put him under scrutiny he couldn't easily evade.

As Ahmed's team departed, the group reconvened at Rafiq's house to plan their next steps. Despite the damage and disruption, a sense of unity held them together, each member focused on the mission ahead.

"We'll need to be more cautious than ever," Ellie said, scanning the group's faces. "Karim won't stop, and we have to be ready for anything. This temple is too important to leave unprotected."

Nadia nodded. "The Ministry's support is invaluable, but it won't stop Karim alone. We need to stay vigilant and continue the work, no matter the obstacles."

That evening, they worked side by side, reconstructing notes and updating records with fresh determination. As the sun dipped below the horizon, casting a golden glow across the desert sands, Ellie felt a renewed commitment to their cause. They had faced Karim's threats, and they remained undeterred. This temple, its guardian spirit, and the legacy it preserved deserved champions who wouldn't falter.

By the time the stars emerged, they had restored much of what had been lost. Standing outside under the vast desert sky, Ellie looked around at her team. They were stronger than before, each of them bound to the temple's story by more than professional duty—it was now a shared mission, one that transcended their own lifetimes.

***

The next morning, the desert dawn brought a crisp stillness that felt almost unnatural. Every sound—the whisper of wind across the sand, the faint clink of equipment—seemed amplified, and the team's movements reflected the tension simmering under the surface. The added security around the site was both a reassurance and a reminder of Karim's lurking presence. Ministry guards moved efficiently among the guard posts set up along the perimeter, their watchful eyes scanning for anything unusual.

As they approached the temple, Ellie couldn't shake the feeling that something was watching them. Her heart pounded as they passed through the barricades, taking in the fortified setup. Ahmed's guards, alert and purposeful, watched their approach, nodding as Ellie and her team passed. For the first time in days, the temple felt genuinely secured.

Simon's hand brushed Ellie's as they walked, offering a subtle reassurance. "This should give Karim some pause," he murmured, his eyes taking in the guards around them. "It's a whole different level of defense now."

Ellie nodded, though her own gaze remained vigilant. "He's always been a step ahead of us," she replied, keeping her voice low. "But this time, he'll have to go through more than us if he tries anything again."

They joined the others at the temple entrance, where Nadia was checking the supplies with quiet efficiency. She nodded to Ellie, her gaze briefly scanning the guards around them before meeting Ellie's eyes.

"The Ministry's set up shifts to monitor the site around the clock," she said in a hushed tone. "We're cleared to resume, but let's keep our documentation brief and take anything significant back with us tonight."

Ellie agreed, the words underscoring the new precautions they'd implemented. They'd carefully prepared secondary records for today's work, choosing only what they needed for immediate field notes and documentation. Anything of value would return to Rafiq's house before nightfall.

Inside, they moved toward the chamber where they'd left their offerings, noting the undisturbed altar and the serene order of the space. Ellie felt a quiet relief seeing it untouched, the offerings of flowers and stones placed with reverence. It was as though this sacred space had evaded Karim's reach, and she hoped it would stay that way.

After spending a moment in quiet reflection, Nadia led them to a narrow corridor branching further into the temple, guiding them toward a section they hadn't explored. Her steps slowed, voice barely above a whisper as she spoke. "The carvings here suggest this part of the temple was sacred, reserved for higher rites and ceremonies."

Ellie's excitement grew, tempered only by the weight of her responsibility. The atmosphere shifted as they ventured deeper, the air turning cooler, heavy with the presence of centuries-old mysteries. The passage narrowed, finally opening into a vast chamber where their flashlights illuminated towering pillars covered in intricate carvings, each pillar telling its own story. Images of robed figures, animals—both real and mythical—and constellations spiraled up the stone, giving the space a solemn, timeless presence.

Layla's breath caught as her light fell on a mural along the far wall. Set apart from the others, it was framed by an archway that stretched from floor to ceiling, its carvings intact and preserved. The mural depicted a central figure, its arms outstretched, while figures knelt in supplication below. Stars and spirals framed the deity's head, forming an arrangement that seemed to pulse with the rhythm of something ancient and powerful.

"This is remarkable," Layla murmured, reaching a hand toward the mural without touching it. "They're not just praying—they're reaching toward the stars. It's as if the deity is part of both earth and sky."

Nadia stepped forward, her expression softened with awe. "Look closely at the constellations. They match some of the ancient Nabatean star patterns. This wasn't just a place of worship; it was a place of communion with something beyond."

Ellie examined the mural, her pulse quickening as the figure's celestial symbolism came into focus. The deity's outstretched arms and the surrounding stars suggested something greater—a cosmic guardian who bridged the earthly and divine. "They may have believed this deity was a link between them and the cosmos," she said, her voice filled with wonder.

Simon studied the mural, nodding slowly. "Perhaps this spirit was more than a protector. It could have been a seer, a guide. The people who built this temple must have felt they were in the presence of something beyond their world."

They documented the mural with meticulous care, photographing every detail and taking notes. Ellie couldn't shake the sensation that they were uncovering more than history—they were walking through the beliefs of an ancient civilization, one that felt vividly alive in these carvings and symbols. She found herself imagining the temple as it must have been: filled with the light of torches, the sound of quiet prayers rising like whispers to the stars.

Nadia motioned for them to continue, leading the way down a sloping passage that opened into a smaller, narrower chamber. Here, the walls were bare, save for a single line of symbols etched near the entrance. The floor was covered in a careful pattern of small, polished stones that spiraled inward, leading to a low, flat slab at the center.

Ellie's heart raced as she took in the scene. "This must have been a ritual space," she murmured. "A place for offerings, maybe even rites of passage."

Nadia's expression grew somber as she examined the stone slab. "If the altar chamber was meant for devotion, then this was where people enacted their beliefs. The stones—they form a symbolic journey to the heart of the temple, a journey toward understanding or enlightenment."

Simon knelt, touching one of the smooth stones in the spiral. "They were chosen carefully. Each stone is unique, polished by hand, as if each one held significance."

They documented the chamber in respectful silence, careful not to disturb the stones or the slab. The room carried a gravity that went beyond mere archaeology; it was a deeply spiritual place, a testament to the people's reverence and connection to the divine.

As they finished, Layla spoke up, her voice barely above a whisper. "It feels as if the temple itself is guiding us, room by room, deeper into something hidden."

Ellie considered her words as they made their way back to the main corridor. The temple did seem to carry them forward, revealing its secrets slowly, like a journey through layers of meaning and faith.

As they prepared to leave for the day, Nadia pulled Ellie aside, her brow furrowed in thought. "Ellie, I think we're on the verge of understanding something profound about this temple. But we need to remain vigilant. Karim is still watching, and I'm certain he won't hesitate to strike again."

Ellie's expression hardened. "Whatever he tries, we'll keep moving forward. This temple holds more than artifacts—it holds a legacy that deserves protection."

They returned to Rafiq's house as the sun dipped low over the horizon. Exhausted but resolute, they prepared for the evening, each member carrying a newfound appreciation for the mysteries hidden within the temple.

But as Ellie settled in for the night, a loud bang echoed from the courtyard. She bolted upright, her heart racing, and exchanged a tense look with Simon. He grabbed his jacket, signaling for her to stay close as they hurried outside.

In the courtyard, Youssef and Rafiq stood with Ahmed's security team, their expressions serious. Youssef gestured toward the outer gate, where a small package lay half-buried in the sand.

"We found this thrown over the wall," Youssef said. "It might be another message from Karim."

Ellie approached cautiously, her stomach twisting with dread. She knelt beside the package, examining it closely. Wrapped in rough paper, it bore a crude drawing in dark ink—a twisted, mocking sketch of the guardian spirit from the temple's mural.

Nadia's face paled with anger as she inspected it. "He's toying with us, daring us to continue. He wants us to know he's close and watching."

Simon placed a hand on Ellie's shoulder, his expression grim. "We need to alert the Ministry and the police. Karim's threats are escalating. He isn't just trying to scare us now—he's actively working to break us."

Ellie felt a surge of determination rise within her. Karim's intimidation was unrelenting, but so was her resolve. The temple, its ancient guardians, and the legacy it embodied deserved protectors who would stand firm. She knew now that they'd been called to this place for a reason.

As they regrouped and reported the incident to the Ministry, Ellie realized they were entering a new phase of their mission. Karim's patience was wearing thin, but their determination was only growing stronger. They would defend this temple and its mysteries—not just with their knowledge and research, but with the fierce conviction that some histories were too sacred to be lost.

That night, as the desert quieted and Ellie lay awake in the safe house, she whispered a silent promise to the guardian spirit, vowing to protect its sanctuary. She knew this journey would demand everything from them, but they would not fail.

A PROFESSOR'S
REVELATION

The following afternoon, Ellie and Simon found themselves navigating the bustling halls of the local university. After the previous night's incident, Nadia had arranged a meeting with Professor Malik, who had become something of a trusted ally—a fount of knowledge and, they hoped, a source of clarity in the increasingly murky waters surrounding their work. His extensive research in regional history, particularly in sacred sites and ancient rites, made him the ideal person to help them understand the deeper meaning of the temple they'd been excavating.

Professor Malik was waiting for them in his office, a modest room lined with bookshelves filled with thick, well-worn tomes and manuscripts. The room's dim lighting and the faint scent of old paper and leather lent it an air of mystery, as though they had stepped into an ancient library rather than a modern academic office.

Malik greeted them warmly, gesturing for them to sit. "Dr. Whitcombe, Dr. Whitcombe," he said, smiling as he shook their hands. "It's a pleasure to see you both again, though I wish it were under less precarious circumstances."

Ellie nodded, taking a seat across from him. "Thank you for meeting with us, Professor Malik. We've uncovered symbols and rituals that are... different from anything we've encountered before. Nadia mentioned you might have insights into their origins."

Malik's expression turned serious, and he leaned forward, his hands steepled thoughtfully. "Nadia was right to send you to me. I've spent much of my career studying the belief systems of the ancient desert cultures. But the temple you're describing, with its star symbols and deity figures... it's unusual. In fact, it's rare enough that I was surprised to hear of it at all. You may have stumbled upon something significant—something connected to a lost order of worship, one not well documented."

Simon exchanged a glance with Ellie, his interest piqued. "A lost order? What exactly do you mean?"

Malik picked up a book from his desk, a worn volume with faded gold lettering along the spine. He flipped to a marked page and handed it to Ellie. She scanned the page, noting drawings of what appeared to be constellations interwoven with figures of robed men holding torches, their arms raised to the sky.

"In ancient times," Malik explained, "there were certain desert tribes who revered what they called *al-Rawi Najm*, 'the Teller of Stars.' This figure was a deity or spirit believed to guide the people through knowledge of the cosmos. The people sought its favor not only for protection but to gain insight into the divine nature of the stars."

Ellie felt a thrill of excitement as she studied the illustrations. "The carvings we found in the temple—it matches this idea of the stars as symbols of divine guidance. The figures kneeling in prayer, reaching toward the stars... it aligns with this idea."

"Exactly," Malik replied, nodding. "But there's more. The Teller of Stars was thought to be a watcher, a silent observer of both human actions and the heavens' movements. Tribes believed it held power to influence fate, both blessing and cursing those who sought its wisdom. Some accounts even suggest that certain rites performed in its temples were meant to bind followers in a protective covenant, a pact that tied them to the deity's guardianship."

Simon leaned forward, visibly captivated. "You're saying that this deity wasn't just worshiped—it was seen as a force of fate itself?"

Malik nodded solemnly. "Yes, exactly. And that may be why the temple you've found feels so... charged. If the people who built it believed they were binding themselves to this spirit, it would explain the intense reverence you described. This temple was likely more than a place of worship. It was an entry point into a cosmic pact."

The weight of Malik's words settled over the room, and Ellie felt a chill despite the warmth. The idea of ancient worshipers making pacts, intertwining their lives and fates with a spirit that observed silently from the heavens—it was hauntingly beautiful, and a little unsettling.

"There's something else I should tell you," Malik said, his tone shifting. He retrieved a small, fragile-looking scroll from his desk, carefully unrolling it to reveal faded text in a script Ellie didn't recognize. "This is one of the few records of *al-Rawi Najm* left intact. It mentions rituals performed at sites like the one you're exploring. But it also includes warnings. They believed that those who entered the temple with impure motives would suffer misfortune. According to these accounts, the Teller of Stars punished those who desecrated its sanctuaries."

Simon exchanged a troubled glance with Ellie. "You're saying that Karim—someone with less-than-pure intentions—could be in danger?"

Malik gave a slight nod. "If these beliefs held any truth for the people of that time, then yes. The deity they worshiped was not one to be trifled with. And if Karim is as relentless as you describe, his motives might have already stirred something at the site."

Ellie felt a strange mix of fear and fascination. She thought of the cave collapse, the unsettling feeling that the temple itself was aware of them. Could there really be a guardian spirit, something ancient and powerful, watching over its sanctuary?

Malik continued, his expression grave. "These records warn of a cycle—a pattern. Those who entered these temples without reverence often met with accidents, strange misfortunes that drove them away or caused them to abandon their quests altogether. It's said that the Teller of Stars could distinguish between those who sought wisdom and those who sought only to exploit."

Ellie took a deep breath, feeling the weight of the revelation settle over her. "So Karim's defilement of the temple might not just be a physical threat to us—it could be a trigger for whatever powers linger in that place."

"Precisely," Malik replied. "I don't wish to instill fear, but I do believe caution is warranted. You're dealing with a site of historical and spiritual significance. The people who worshiped there held beliefs that shaped their lives, and they would have taken great pains to protect their sanctuary from intrusion."

Simon's face was thoughtful as he looked at Malik. "We've already been extremely careful, but it sounds like we need to take additional steps. We can't afford to underestimate this."

Malik nodded. "And I would also recommend keeping your findings as private as possible, especially in light of Karim's persistence. If he learns the true depth of this temple's significance, he may go to even greater lengths to gain control."

Ellie agreed, feeling a surge of protectiveness for the temple and its secrets. "Thank you, Professor Malik. This insight changes everything."

As they made to leave, Malik held up a hand, his face softening. "One last thing. Remember that the ancient people believed in the power of intention. They thought that pure-hearted seekers were offered protection by the very forces they revered. Perhaps, in honoring this temple, you may find yourselves under the same guardianship."

Ellie and Simon left his office with a profound sense of both awe and caution. They knew now that they weren't just archaeologists documenting history—they were custodians of something far deeper, something that held power even in the modern age.

As they walked through the bustling streets back toward Rafiq's house, they discussed the implications of Malik's warning. The ancient records were more than just folklore; they were guides, left behind by a people who'd understood the significance of respecting powerful forces. Karim's disregard for the temple's sanctity could be his undoing—but they had to be vigilant.

Back at Rafiq's, they gathered the team, sharing the revelations from Professor Malik's research. Nadia listened intently, her face growing serious as Ellie described the Teller of Stars and its role as both protector and punisher.

"It makes sense," Nadia said thoughtfully. "The temple has always felt like more than just a historical site. There's a reverence that's almost... tangible."

Amir nodded, looking contemplative. "It might also explain why the locals have always stayed away. Perhaps they sensed that this place demands respect."

Simon added, "Malik also advised us to be more cautious with our findings. If Karim catches wind of what we've uncovered, he may go to any lengths to take control. We have to be strategic and keep our discoveries as contained as possible."

They spent the evening planning how to limit their exposure, deciding to keep new discoveries offsite and implement stricter controls over access to sensitive information. Youssef offered to increase his local contacts' involvement, ensuring they had additional eyes monitoring the site for any unusual activity.

As the night grew late, Ellie and Simon sat quietly in Rafiq's courtyard, watching the stars above. The revelation of the Teller of Stars weighed heavily on Ellie's mind. She felt as if they'd only scratched the surface of a legacy that transcended centuries. Malik's warnings had been clear, and she could feel the responsibility settle over her.

"Simon," she said quietly, glancing up at the constellation-laden sky, "do you think there's truth in Malik's theory? That the Teller of Stars might actually protect this place?"

Simon looked thoughtful, his gaze fixed on the heavens. "I think there's more to this world than we understand. And maybe, by honoring what we've found, we're connecting with something bigger than ourselves. Either way, I feel like we're part of something profound."

Ellie nodded, feeling a mix of wonder and resolve. The temple, with its secrets and its ancient guardians, was more than a site on a map. It was a bridge to the past, one that demanded both reverence and protection.

She leaned against Simon, their eyes turned to the heavens. Whatever the coming days held, she knew they were ready. The stars above seemed to watch them in silence, and she couldn't help but feel they were being guided by forces as old as the earth itself.

After their conversation with Professor Malik, Nadia suggested a short break, knowing that a few days away from the temple site might offer Ellie and Simon some much-needed rest and perspective. The relentless focus on their work—and the mounting tension with Karim—had left them drained. A short interlude would allow them to regroup and experience the historical treasures Amman had to offer. And, as Nadia pointed out, a visible presence around the city might help throw Karim off their trail, if only temporarily.

The next morning, Ellie and Simon found themselves in a bustling Amman street, surrounded by the hum of daily life. Despite the shadow of their work and the discreet security guards who trailed them at a distance, Ellie felt a thrill of excitement as they walked hand-in-hand. Here, away from the temple, she could almost relax, letting herself be captivated by the sounds, scents, and colors of the city.

Their first stop was the ancient Roman Theater, an enormous structure nestled against a hillside in the heart of Amman. The theater was a remnant of the city's time as Philadelphia, one of the Decapolis cities, and its wide stone seats fanned out in concentric circles around the stage, where actors and orators once captivated audiences.

Simon gazed up at the towering stone seats, his expression contemplative. "It's humbling, isn't it?" he said, his voice reverent. "To think that people sat here nearly two thousand years ago, watching performances, gathering to hear news from across the empire."

Ellie nodded, letting her fingers trail along the smooth, cool stone. "It's like touching a piece of a world we can never fully understand, but somehow we're still connected to it." She looked over at him with a smile. "And maybe it's a reminder that our work is part of a much bigger story."

They wandered through the theater, admiring the ancient architecture and watching locals who had gathered to socialize, take photos, or simply enjoy the view. The vibrant hum of voices, laughter, and occasional street vendors made the experience even richer, a reminder that history and the present were forever entwined.

After the theater, they strolled through Amman's Citadel, one of the city's highest points and a place that offered panoramic views of the city's sprawling neighborhoods. Here, amidst the ruins of the Temple of Hercules and Byzantine churches, Ellie felt a moment of quiet reflection. The Temple of Hercules loomed nearby, with its towering columns reaching toward the sky, an ancient marvel that had withstood centuries of change and turmoil.

Simon glanced around, his eyes soft with admiration. "This place has seen empires rise and fall. It's amazing that it's still here, a witness to all that's come and gone."

They moved through the ruins, pausing to read plaques that described the different structures, the changes each had undergone over centuries. The stones, weathered and worn, seemed to carry the weight of countless lives and stories. Ellie could almost imagine the temple in its prime—priests and worshippers moving about, offerings laid at the feet of statues, prayers whispered to gods who had long since faded from memory.

As they walked, she felt a renewed sense of purpose. Protecting the temple back at the dig site was more than just about preserving history—it was about honoring the lives and beliefs of the people who had built it.

After an afternoon immersed in the wonders of Amman, they stopped at a small, family-owned café nestled in a quiet side street. The café was adorned with traditional Jordanian decor: woven rugs on the walls, intricate lanterns casting warm light, and the scent of cardamom and mint wafting through the air.

They ordered plates of mezze, an array of small dishes that included hummus, baba ghanoush, tabbouleh, and falafel. Ellie felt her shoulders relax as she tasted each dish, savoring the fresh flavors and the rich spices that seemed to reflect the vibrant spirit of the city. Simon, too, seemed content, a faint smile on his face as he sampled the dishes.

"This was exactly what we needed," Ellie said, her voice soft as she gazed out at the bustling street beyond the café's window. "It's easy to lose sight of why we do this work, but days like this remind me of the beauty and resilience of history. Amman is alive with it."

Simon nodded, taking a sip of his strong Arabic coffee. "And it's humbling to see how people continue to honor their past. This city has adapted to the modern world, but it's never lost its connection to where it came from. I think it's a lesson for us, too—to honor the past while moving forward."

After their meal, they continued to explore the city's labyrinthine streets, wandering through the bustling souks. Stalls overflowed with colorful fabrics, intricately patterned ceramics, and handmade jewelry, each item telling its own story. The shopkeepers greeted them with warm smiles, eager to share the origins of their wares and offer samples of fragrant spices and dried fruits.

Ellie's gaze lingered on a beautifully crafted silver pendant, etched with an intricate design that reminded her of the symbols they'd found at the temple. The shopkeeper, noticing her interest, explained that the design was a traditional protective charm, believed to guard against misfortune and bring blessings to those who wore it.

Without hesitation, Simon purchased the pendant for her, fastening it around her neck with a gentle smile. "Consider it a reminder," he said, "of why we're here, and of the power that history holds."

Ellie touched the pendant, feeling a warmth that went beyond its simple design. She knew that in the days to come, the symbol would remind her of their work, the ancient forces they sought to protect, and the enduring strength of human belief.

As evening descended, they returned to Rafiq's house, where the quiet offered a contrast to the bustling city streets they'd left behind. Youssef and their security team had remained unobtrusive, keeping a watchful eye but allowing the Whitcombes their space to enjoy the day. Despite the underlying caution, Ellie felt refreshed, her mind clearer, her purpose reaffirmed.

That night, as they sat outside under the starlit sky, the weight of Professor Malik's revelations hung between them, tempered now by a sense of renewed resolve. Ellie gazed up at the constellations, thinking of the Teller of Stars and the ancient people who had worshiped it. The pendant Simon had bought felt warm against her skin, and she felt a strange comfort, as though the temple's guardian spirit was somehow watching over them.

"It's strange," she said, breaking the comfortable silence. "Being away from the dig, exploring Amman... it's helped me understand why the ancient people chose the Teller of Stars as their guide. There's so much power in the past. It gives you strength, even in the present."

Simon nodded, his gaze thoughtful. "Maybe that's what we've been missing. We've been so focused on the danger from Karim that we forgot to let the history itself guide us. We're not just uncovering artifacts—we're uncovering a way of seeing the world, a perspective that gave those people purpose. And I think it can do the same for us."

Ellie leaned against him, feeling his steady presence as she looked out over the darkened landscape. The day in Amman had reminded her that history was more than relics and ruins. It was a living presence, one that connected people across centuries, across cultures. The Teller of Stars, the guardian spirit, was not merely a symbol but a reminder of the strength and resilience that came from honoring what was sacred.

As they finally turned in for the night, Ellie felt a profound peace settle within her. They would return to the temple with a renewed understanding, carrying not just Professor Malik's cautionary advice but the spirit of Amman itself—a spirit that had endured through centuries, standing steadfast in the face of change and challenge.

The city had offered them not just a respite, but a reminder of their purpose, a purpose that extended beyond archaeology. It was about protecting the enduring legacy of belief, resilience, and the unbreakable bond between past and present.

19

BONDING IN THE DESERT

The evening breeze drifted over the desert, cooling the sands and casting a peaceful hush across the dunes. Nadia's suggestion to spend an evening together, away from the demands of the dig, had been welcomed eagerly by everyone. After weeks of relentless work—and the constant shadow of Karim—the team needed this time to unwind and appreciate the beauty of the desert, no matter how guarded they had to remain.

They gathered around a small fire, its warm glow illuminating their faces and casting long shadows across the sand. Ellie leaned back against a low stone, content to listen to Youssef, who had just finished a thrilling local legend about a Djinn who protected travelers respectful of the desert's secrets. The group had fallen into laughter, all eyes on Youssef as he recounted the story with an intensity that made even Amir chuckle.

"Alright, who's next?" Layla asked, plucking a few playful notes on her ukulele, a new tune she'd been experimenting with. "Come on, there must be more stories here. Nadia? Amir?"

Nadia, seated across from Ellie, glanced up, her face softening with a hint of a smile. "Alright," she said, her voice warm. "But I'll warn you, my story isn't quite as charming as being stranded on a Greek island."

Simon leaned forward, grinning. "We're all ears, Nadia. Don't hold back!"

Nadia chuckled, her eyes reflecting the flickering firelight. "Well, back when I was still a graduate student, I was part of a dig in Petra. It was my first major expedition, and I was beyond excited, maybe too eager for my own good. One night, after a day of grueling work, I snuck out of camp to go exploring alone."

Amir raised an eyebrow, feigning shock. "Our responsible Nadia? Sneaking out?"

Nadia laughed. "Yes, I know. You wouldn't think it. But I had heard rumors from a local guide about a hidden passageway near the Monastery. So, in the dead of night, I grabbed a flashlight and went off on my own to find it."

Layla's eyes widened. "Did you find it?"

"Oh, I found something alright," Nadia replied, her expression sheepish. "I got hopelessly lost! One wrong turn, and suddenly I had no idea where I was. To make matters worse, my flashlight died."

The group gasped, leaning in closer as Nadia continued.

"So there I was, fumbling around in the dark with nothing but the sound of my own footsteps and the distant calls of jackals to keep me company. I must have wandered for hours, convinced I was about to become a permanent part of Petra. Finally, just as I was about to accept my fate, I heard voices. A local family had set up camp nearby, and they found me, wandering like a ghost. They gave me water, scolded me for my foolishness, and brought me back to camp."

Ellie laughed, picturing Nadia's stern rescuers and her embarrassed return to camp. "I bet you were a sight to behold."

Nadia nodded, laughing softly. "I must have looked half-mad by then. My supervisor, an older professor who had no patience for nonsense, just looked at me and said, 'Miss al-Masri, let this be a lesson. Archaeology requires respect for the unknown and the humility to know when to ask for help.'"

Simon chuckled, raising his cup in salute. "And I bet you never went exploring alone again."

"Never," Nadia confirmed, her tone playful. "Lesson learned. Respect the desert and its mysteries, or they'll humble you fast."

Amir smiled, crossing his arms over his knees. "I can't picture you getting lost, Nadia. You're practically a compass with legs."

Nadia waved a dismissive hand. "That night, I was as lost as anyone could be. The desert has a way of reminding you that you're small—no matter how much you think you know."

They sat in reflective silence for a moment, the soft crackle of the fire filling the quiet. Layla plucked a gentle melody on her ukulele, setting a relaxing rhythm that seemed to blend with the distant hum of the desert.

Amir cleared his throat, drawing everyone's attention. "Alright, I suppose it's my turn. It's not as dramatic as Nadia's tale, but it's a lesson in overconfidence nonetheless."

Ellie gave him an encouraging nod, smiling. "We're all listening, Amir."

He settled back, a wry grin tugging at his lips. "A few years ago, I was leading a group of foreign students through Wadi Rum. It was their first time in the desert, and they were excited but also a bit nervous. I decided to show off a little—make them feel like they were in safe hands, you know?"

Youssef laughed knowingly, shaking his head. "Showing off never ends well, my friend."

"Truer words," Amir agreed, laughing. "So I'm telling them all these things about reading tracks in the sand, navigating by the stars, making them think I could do this with my eyes closed. We set up camp, and as night falls, I confidently tell them we're camped in a 'jackal-free zone.'"

Layla snorted. "I didn't know jackals respected boundaries like that."

"Neither did I," Amir replied, shaking his head in amusement. "But I wanted to sound like I was in control. Not ten minutes later, as I'm assuring everyone there are no jackals, we hear howling—close enough to make everyone jump."

The group laughed, picturing Amir's students' reactions.

"Next thing I know, one of the students is practically on my back, asking if we're about to be attacked. I had to admit that jackals, unlike yours truly, don't actually respect my opinion on where they should roam."

The laughter grew louder, echoing across the desert. Amir chuckled, holding up his hands. "So much for the fearless guide. After that, I let the desert speak for itself."

Ellie laughed, shaking her head. "So much for overconfidence. The desert doesn't let anyone show off for long, does it?"

Amir grinned. "It doesn't, indeed. That night, I learned that humility is the best companion out here."

The firelight flickered as the group settled into a comfortable silence, each person lost in thoughts of their own. Ellie leaned into Simon, feeling an overwhelming sense of gratitude for this evening, this group, and the chance to simply be present in a way that was rare amid the intensity of their work.

Ellie felt a renewed sense of camaraderie among them, and the tales shared under the starlit sky reminded her of how deeply their paths had intertwined. She reached over and squeezed Simon's hand, feeling his warmth.

"So," Simon said after a moment, casting a glance around the group, "does anyone else feel like they're back at summer camp? Campfire stories, snacks, only the occasional wild animal to keep things interesting?"

Layla grinned, strumming a playful tune. "I'll admit, it's got that feeling. The only thing missing is the ghost story to make us jump."

Youssef's eyes sparkled mischievously. "Oh, I've got one of those too, but I'd hate to keep you all awake."

Amir laughed, raising his hands. "I think we've had enough nighttime spooks. I'd rather go to bed without hearing about desert ghosts, thank you."

But before they could protest, Youssef began a tale of an ancient specter, rumored to haunt lost travelers in the desert, appearing as a lone figure wandering through the dunes on moonlit nights. He delivered the story with such suspense that even Ellie, who knew it was all in fun, felt the hair on her arms rise as she imagined the lonely desert figure. When he finished, a chill lingered in the air, the firelight casting eerie shadows across their faces.

"That," Layla said, her voice breathless, "was terrifyingly good."

They laughed, but each of them cast a wary glance out into the night as if half-expecting to see Youssef's specter prowling the sands. Eventually, the laughter faded, replaced by a deep sense of calm. Ellie gazed up at the vast desert sky, the stars stretched out like endless pinpricks of light.

As she leaned against Simon, her heart filled with a renewed love for this life of exploration. In this moment, under the wide expanse of stars, she remembered the thrill of discovery that had first brought her and Simon together, the passion that had fueled every adventure since. She looked up at him, feeling as though she could see the young man she'd fallen in love with all those years ago.

Simon smiled down at her, the same sense of affection mirrored in his gaze. "Ellie," he murmured, "we may be older and a bit wiser, but I think there's still a part of us that's just as adventurous as ever."

Ellie smiled, leaning up to kiss his cheek. "Then let's keep being adventurers."

Absolutely! Here's an extended continuation, adding more warmth, dialogue, and connection-building among the team as they linger together in the desert night. This will allow for even deeper bonding moments, some humor, and reflections that set the stage for the challenges they'll face together in the coming days.

As the laughter faded, a gentle stillness settled over the group, each person lost in their own thoughts. The fire crackled softly, casting a flickering glow on their faces as they leaned back, relaxing into the warmth of companionship. Above them, the stars stretched endlessly, seeming almost close enough to touch.

Layla resumed her strumming, playing a softer, slower tune as they all took in the beauty of the desert night. Ellie watched her, appreciating the way Layla's music added a sense of magic to the evening, as if they were all part of some ancient ritual under the stars.

Nadia broke the silence, her tone reflective. "You know, I think this has been one of the most unexpected journeys of my life. When I started this project, I knew it would

be challenging, but I never imagined all of you would become... well, like family."

Ellie nodded, touched by Nadia's words. "It does feel that
way, doesn't it? Like we were meant to come together."

Simon glanced around the group, a smile tugging at his
lips. "I think we all know that real friendships aren't built
on perfect circumstances. They're forged through challenges—and a little bit of chaos."

Amir laughed, his voice warm. "If that's the case, we
should be closer than ever with all the chaos we've had
lately."

Youssef, who had been quietly sipping his tea, chuckled
and raised his cup in mock toast. "To chaos, then. And to
good friends who make it bearable."

They lifted their cups and bottles, a sense of joy and
unity filling the air. Layla continued playing, her eyes
closed as her fingers danced across the strings, lost in her
own world. The melody seemed to echo across the sands,
weaving itself into the fabric of the desert night.

Youssef lowered his cup, looking out at the starlit horizon. "You know," he said thoughtfully, "the desert is both
a blessing and a challenge. It teaches you patience, humility... and how to face the unknown without fear."

Ellie watched him, captivated by the wisdom in his
words. "I think we've all learned a little bit of that out here,"
she replied. "The desert has a way of stripping away everything unnecessary, leaving only what truly matters."

Layla looked up, her fingers still strumming. "What
truly matters," she repeated softly. "It's funny, but I think

the desert has taught me more in the past few weeks than any classroom ever could."

Simon smiled, nodding. "I think that's the beauty of history—and of places like this. They remind us that we're part of something much bigger. We may be here for a moment, but the past... it stretches on forever."

Ellie felt Simon's words resonate deeply within her. Here, under the vast expanse of stars, she was reminded of the significance of the temple and the responsibility they had to protect it. This mission had become more than just an academic pursuit; it was a calling, a connection to the lives and beliefs of those who had come before.

Nadia looked over at Amir, a mischievous glint in her eye. "Speaking of what truly matters," she teased, "Amir, didn't you once tell me about your very first job as a guide?"

Amir groaned, shaking his head. "Oh no, Nadia, not that story."

The group perked up, sensing the promise of more laughter. "Come on, Amir," Layla coaxed. "Now you have to tell us!"

Amir sighed, throwing his hands up in mock resignation. "Fine. But I'll deny every word of it if you bring it up later."

He leaned back, a grin spreading across his face as he began. "So, back when I was still learning the ropes, I got hired to lead a group of college students through Wadi Rum. I was nervous, of course, but I didn't want them to know that. I was trying to be the confident, seasoned guide."

He paused, shaking his head with a wry smile. "We had just set up camp when I realized I'd forgotten one of the most important things—water. I'd left a whole crate of it back at the drop-off point."

Ellie stifled a laugh, covering her mouth. "Oh no..."

"Oh yes," Amir said, laughing along with her. "Of course, I didn't want to admit I'd forgotten it, so I spent half the night trying to ration what little we had left, hoping nobody would notice. By the time I finally owned up to it, they were all too tired to care—and I had to listen to their complaints the entire walk back the next day."

Layla was practically doubled over in laughter. "Lesson learned, I hope?"

Amir held up his hands. "Lesson learned, absolutely. Now I triple-check for supplies, especially water. I never want to go through that again."

They shared another round of laughter, the joy and ease of the moment washing over them like a balm. Ellie found herself looking at each person around the fire, feeling a profound sense of gratitude for this group of friends who had become like family.

The stars were bright overhead, stretching across the sky in a vast, glittering canopy. Ellie tilted her head back, taking in the constellations that had guided travelers and wanderers for centuries. In the quiet, she could almost feel the presence of those who had come before them, bound by the same desert sands and starlit skies.

Youssef leaned forward, his voice softer now. "You know, I believe the desert brings people together for a reason. It's a place of solitude, yes, but also of connection. It's as if the desert sees something in each of us that we're meant to learn from each other."

Simon nodded thoughtfully. "It's true. I think that's what makes this journey so special. We've come here from different paths, different lives, but somehow, we're all connected through this shared purpose."

Ellie squeezed Simon's hand, feeling the truth in his words. This journey had been unexpected in many ways, but she wouldn't trade it for anything. Here, surrounded by friends and a vast, ancient landscape, she felt a deep sense of belonging.

As the night grew darker, the conversations began to quiet, and they fell into a peaceful silence. Layla's ukulele was the only sound, a gentle lullaby that drifted across the sands. Ellie leaned her head against Simon's shoulder, feeling his warmth and strength beside her.

After a while, Nadia glanced at her watch and stretched, yawning. "Well, as much as I'd love to stay up all night, we should probably get some sleep. Tomorrow brings us back to the temple, and I'd like us all well-rested for whatever discoveries await."

One by one, they rose from their spots around the fire, gathering their belongings. As they began to disperse toward their tents, Ellie lingered, taking one last look at the vast desert around them, the stars shimmering brightly above.

Simon stood beside her, wrapping an arm around her shoulders. "You ready to call it a night?"

Ellie nodded, leaning into him. "Yes. But tonight feels special. I think it's one of those nights we'll remember for a long time. There's something about this place—it's like it has a heartbeat of its own."

Simon looked out over the starlit landscape, his gaze soft and reflective. "It does. And I think it's brought us all here for a reason. I feel closer to everything—history, our purpose, even... us."

They shared a quiet smile, then walked hand-in-hand to their tent, feeling the warmth of the night settle around them. Inside, as they lay down on their sleeping mats, Ellie reached over, her hand finding his.

"I feel like we're back to our old selves out here," she whispered, tracing a finger along his palm. "It reminds me of our early days—just us, with no plan but to see what the world would show us."

Simon smiled, turning to face her. "Then let's make this another chapter of our adventure." He leaned in, pressing a soft kiss to her forehead before resting his hand on her cheek. "I don't think I ever really stopped falling in love with you, Ellie. And I'm grateful for every day we get to live out this journey together."

Ellie's heart swelled as she tilted her head up, meeting his gaze before brushing her lips against his. It was a gentle, lingering kiss, one that held all the memories, the laughter, and the love they'd shared through the years. In that moment, the world around them faded, leaving only the two of them, bound by a love as timeless as the desert.

They lay together in a comfortable silence, their fingers intertwined, feeling the closeness that only the shared wonder of the unknown could bring. Outside, the desert whispered around them, its ancient stories blending with their own, carrying them toward whatever lay ahead.

And as sleep finally took them, Ellie knew that this journey was far from over—there were more stories to uncover, more mysteries to explore, and more moments like this to cherish.

THE TREASURE MAP

The sun was beginning its descent, casting warm, amber light over the desert landscape as the team gathered near the entrance to the site. They had spent the afternoon cataloging their finds and preparing new notes, but as Nadia approached, her expression held something new: a quiet intensity and anticipation. In her hands, she held a worn, leather-bound case.

"I've been waiting for the right moment to show you all this," Nadia began, her voice steady yet carrying an undertone of excitement. "This map fragment has been in my possession for years, but until now, I wasn't certain of its significance."

Layla's eyes widened as she leaned in closer, glancing from Nadia to the case. "A map? But... how does it connect to what we've been finding?"

Nadia took a deep breath and opened the case, revealing a parchment so old that its edges were frayed and faded. Symbols ran across its surface, winding like veins toward what appeared to be a central location marked by a distinct emblem—a symbol that, Ellie and Simon immediately recognized, bore a striking resemblance to one found on the silver disc they had unearthed earlier.

"This map fragment was discovered in a private collection," Nadia explained, her eyes scanning the team's eager faces. "A collector came across it in a market and brought it to me, curious about its origins. But without context, it was only a curiosity. Now, with everything we've uncovered here, I believe it's something far more valuable."

Ellie moved closer to inspect the map, her heart racing as she traced the delicate lines with her eyes. "These markings... they look almost identical to the carvings we found on the disc. And the way they're arranged here..." She trailed off, a mixture of wonder and disbelief coloring her voice. "It's as if this map is guiding us, like a path."

Simon joined her, squinting at the faded symbols. "And it's not just a straightforward path. See here?" He pointed to what appeared to be a series of intricate patterns surrounding the central symbol. "This looks like it's deliberately meant to conceal something—a hidden chamber, maybe, or an area of great significance."

Amir, who had been silent, studying the map with his usual attentiveness, finally spoke. "If this map truly leads to a chamber, then it's no ordinary find. Whatever lies there could be hidden for a reason—perhaps a religious site or a place reserved for only the most sacred of rituals."

Layla's face brightened, her eyes wide with the possibilities. "It could be a temple, or even a burial site of a revered figure. This might be the missing piece of our puzzle."

As they examined the map, an air of urgency began to settle over the group. Each line, each faded symbol seemed to pull them deeper, igniting the spark of discovery within them all. But even as their excitement grew, Ellie sensed something else—a shadow that seemed to loom larger than the desert's vastness.

They had barely made it past the initial rush of realization when Nadia cleared her throat, her expression turning grave. "There's something you all need to know. We're not the only ones who might be aware of this map."

Simon's gaze sharpened. "You mean Karim."

Nadia nodded, the weight of her concern evident. "Karim has ties to the underground trade in antiquities. The more we uncover, the more he realizes we're close to something valuable. He's been watching our every move, and I wouldn't put it past him to have some of his associates nearby, waiting for any sign of opportunity."

Ellie felt a chill run down her spine as she looked at the map once more, the symbols now carrying an added sense of danger. The relics they were working to protect could be in jeopardy, and their mission had suddenly become as much about preserving Jordan's cultural heritage as it was about personal safety.

Amir's eyes narrowed, his protective instincts kicking in. "Then we need to proceed with utmost caution. We have no idea how far Karim is willing to go, and we can't underestimate him. If he sees us getting closer, he'll stop at nothing to interfere."

Simon looked to the rest of the team, his face filled with determination. "We'll have to work fast and stay under the radar. This isn't just an academic pursuit anymore; it's a race against time."

Nadia, seeming to anticipate Simon's urgency, began outlining the plans for the days ahead. "We'll split up tasks to avoid drawing too much attention to one location. Ellie and Layla, I want you both to document and photograph the map meticulously. Amir and Simon, focus on preparing the gear we'll need if we decide to move toward the next site."

As they divided up responsibilities, the energy among them shifted—no longer was it the lighthearted excitement of discovery. Now, each step was tempered by the knowledge of the danger they faced. The map they held was more than just a clue to hidden history; it was a key to something that powerful forces wanted to control.

They worked through the evening, taking turns analyzing the map and transcribing its symbols. Layla carefully photographed each section, while Ellie sketched the lines onto her notepad, reconstructing the map piece by piece.

As the night wore on, Ellie's mind wandered, recalling each close encounter they'd had with Karim's men and the escalating risk he posed. She glanced at Simon, who was focused on gathering tools and organizing their supplies. Their eyes met briefly, and in that unspoken exchange, she could sense that he felt it too—their journey was shifting from an academic exploration into a high-stakes mission.

Hours later, with the map documented and plans laid out for the next steps, the team gathered once more. They sat in a tight circle, the weight of what lay ahead settling on them.

Nadia, sensing the tension, spoke up. "This is likely our last quiet moment before things get difficult. If we find what I suspect this map leads to, it could change everything we know about Jordan's history. But we have to stay vigilant. Karim will be watching, and if he catches any hint of our destination..."

Amir, his voice calm but resolute, interjected. "We'll handle it. We're not alone in this." He looked around at the others, his gaze lingering on each of them. "Whatever happens, we're in this together."

Ellie nodded, feeling a swell of pride and gratitude for the friends and allies who had become like family on this journey. "And if this map does lead us to a hidden chamber or relics, we'll protect them at all costs. We owe it to the people who came before us and to the ones who will inherit this history after us."

As the team packed up their materials, the tension between excitement and fear hung heavily in the air. They knew that Karim wouldn't rest until he had his prize, and every step they took brought them closer to his crosshairs. But they also knew that this was the adventure they had come for—the chance to uncover history and protect it from those who sought to exploit it.

Just before they parted for the night, Simon turned to the group, his face serious. "Get some rest, everyone. Tomorrow, we follow the map, and who knows what we'll find."

Ellie shared a look with Simon, her heart pounding with a mixture of anticipation and dread. Whatever awaited them was just beyond the next horizon, hidden within the desert's silent sands.

And as she lay awake that night, the map's cryptic lines etched into her memory, she knew they were on the brink of a discovery that would change all of their lives—one that they would protect, no matter the cost.

THROUGH THE CANYONS

The sky was just beginning to lighten as Ellie, Simon, Nadia, and the rest of the team prepared to leave the hidden chamber. After the close call with Karim the previous day, they knew he'd be back with reinforcements, determined to claim the treasure for himself. The narrow passage to the hidden sanctuary had to be sealed, at least temporarily, to buy them time.

"We can't stay here," Amir whispered urgently, glancing over his shoulder as if expecting Karim's shadow to appear at any moment. "If Karim's smart, he'll have us surrounded by sundown."

Nadia's face was tense but resolute. "He's more than smart—he's ruthless. But if we take the canyon path, we can avoid him. It's tricky terrain, but we know these lands better than he does."

Ellie nodded, her heart pounding as she considered their options. They had little time, and Karim was undoubtedly gathering his men for an all-out pursuit. They couldn't afford to be trapped.

Youssef had prepared the vehicles, which were parked behind a natural stone outcrop that provided a bit of cover from prying eyes. He gestured toward the path ahead. "The canyons will be our best bet. The network is confusing, full of twists and narrow passages that Karim's men won't be able to navigate as quickly."

The group quickly gathered their essential supplies, double-checking that the most critical artifacts and records were safely packed. Ellie glanced over at Simon, who gave her a reassuring nod. Despite the danger, she felt a thrill of excitement—a reminder of why they had embarked on this journey in the first place.

"Let's go," Simon said, his voice steady. "And let's hope the desert favors us today."

They piled into the vehicles, Youssef taking the lead with Ellie and Simon seated behind him. Nadia, Amir, and Layla followed in the second vehicle, their faces grim but determined. As they set off, Ellie could feel the adrenaline coursing through her veins, heightening her senses. Every turn, every shadow felt charged with tension.

The canyons rose around them as they drove deeper into the rugged landscape. Towering rock walls loomed on either side, narrowing the path to a winding ribbon of sand

and stone. The only sounds were the hum of the engines and the occasional skitter of rocks as they bounced down the cliffs above.

The group navigated through sharp turns and steep inclines, Youssef handling the wheel with expertise. Ellie glanced over her shoulder, her gaze scanning the canyon behind them. So far, there was no sign of Karim—but she knew better than to let her guard down.

Just as they rounded a bend, the unmistakable echo of engines reverberated through the canyon walls. Ellie's stomach dropped as she realized Karim's men were closing in fast.

"They're right behind us!" Layla shouted over the radio, her voice tense with fear.

Youssef pressed his foot down on the accelerator, his expression grim. "Hold tight! The path's about to get rough."

They barreled down the narrow canyon, the walls closing in as they navigated a series of sharp turns. Dust billowed up around them, clouding their vision, but Youssef pressed on, his hands steady on the wheel.

"Youssef, do you know a way out?" Simon asked, his voice tight with urgency.

Youssef nodded, his eyes fixed on the winding path ahead. "There's a fork up ahead—one path leads to the open desert, but it's too exposed. We'll take the left path through the labyrinth. It's riskier, but Karim's men won't be able to follow us closely."

Ellie clenched her fists, feeling the pressure of each second ticking by as they sped through the canyon. She glanced over at Simon, who gave her a reassuring smile, his hand reaching over to squeeze hers.

The fork in the canyon loomed ahead, and Youssef swerved hard to the left, taking the narrower path. The rock walls closed in, casting deep shadows over the vehicles as they maneuvered through the maze-like canyons. It was as if the desert itself had conspired to keep them hidden, concealing them in its intricate web of stone.

Just when Ellie allowed herself to hope they had lost Karim's men, the roar of engines sounded again—closer this time. She glanced back, spotting two dark vehicles in pursuit, their headlights cutting through the dust.

"They're gaining on us!" Amir's voice crackled through the radio, filled with alarm.

Youssef gritted his teeth, his gaze focused on the treacherous path ahead. "Hold on! This is going to get bumpy."

He swerved sharply to avoid a rockslide, the tires skidding on loose gravel as they veered down a steep slope. The team braced themselves, clinging to the sides of the vehicle as they hurtled down the incline. Behind them, one of Karim's vehicles tried to mimic the maneuver, but lost control, careening into the canyon wall in a burst of dust and debris.

"One down," Simon muttered under his breath, though his face remained tense. "But the others won't be far behind."

As they pressed on, the canyons grew tighter, forcing the vehicles to slow as they navigated the narrow twists and turns. Ellie could feel the heat rising, the sun climbing higher, casting harsh light over the jagged rocks. Karim's remaining vehicle was still in pursuit, its headlights flashing in the rearview mirror like a predatory glare.

"Youssef," Nadia's voice crackled over the radio. "Do you think we can lose them in the next ravine?"

"Maybe," Youssef replied, his voice low. "There's a passage up ahead that leads into a dead-end. If we can make it there and turn off the engines, we might be able to stay hidden."

As they neared the ravine, Ellie could feel her pulse racing, her heart pounding in her chest. This was a risky gamble, but it was the only chance they had to escape Karim's relentless pursuit.

Youssef maneuvered the vehicle around a final bend and into the narrow passage. They came to a stop, cutting the engine and plunging them into silence. Ellie held her breath, straining to listen as the sound of Karim's vehicle drew nearer. The canyon walls seemed to close in around them, the tension thick in the air.

For several agonizing moments, they waited, crouched in silence as Karim's vehicle roared past the ravine, the sound gradually fading as he continued further down the canyon.

They exhaled as one, the relief palpable. Youssef waited a few more moments before he restarted the engine, guiding them carefully out of the ravine and back onto the main path. The desert stretched before them, open and vast, and Ellie felt a flicker of hope rise within her. They'd escaped—at least for now.

"We need to find cover," Nadia said, her voice filled with urgency. "Karim will double back once he realizes we're not ahead of him. Let's make for the cliffs on the other side of the ridge."

They navigated through the remaining canyons, their speed tempered by the need for caution. As they reached the cliffs, Youssef guided them toward a secluded outcrop sheltered by large boulders. Here, they parked, stepping out of the vehicles and gathering in the shade, their breaths ragged as the adrenaline began to fade.

Layla looked over at Ellie, her face pale but her eyes fierce. "That was close. Too close."

Ellie nodded, feeling the weight of their narrow escape settle over her. "But we made it. And as long as we stay one step ahead, we'll finish this journey together."

Simon looked out over the canyon, his gaze steely. "Karim's not going to stop. He knows we're close to something big, and he'll keep coming for us until he gets it."

Nadia placed a hand on his shoulder, her expression resolute. "Then we'll keep fighting. We've come too far to turn back now."

Youssef nodded, his eyes scanning the horizon. "We'll need to keep moving. Karim will search every canyon until he finds us."

Amir reached into his pack, pulling out the map fragment they had recovered. "The map shows another path—a way through the cliffs that leads to a hidden valley. If we can reach it, we might find the last piece of the puzzle. But we'll have to go on foot; it's too narrow for the vehicles."

Ellie felt a surge of determination as she looked around at the team, their faces weary but unyielding. They were in this together, bound by a shared purpose that had only grown stronger through each danger they had faced.

"Then let's go," she said, her voice firm. "We're not backing down. Whatever Karim wants, we'll make sure he never finds it."

With renewed resolve, they gathered their supplies and set off on foot, weaving through the narrow cliffs, each step bringing them closer to the valley—and, they hoped, to the secrets that lay within. The desert loomed around them, a silent witness to their journey, as they pressed forward, ready to face whatever lay ahead.

Absolutely, here's the continuation of Chapter Twenty-One, as the team finds themselves navigating even more perilous terrain on foot, dodging threats and edging closer to their goal—all while Karim and his men continue to close in.

The heat of the day pressed down as they wound through the narrow passages of the canyon on foot, carrying only what they needed. Shadows pooled between the cliff walls, providing some respite from the blazing sun, but the rugged terrain and the constant threat of Karim's men added an intensity that kept their senses on high alert.

Ellie moved beside Simon, her breaths coming in steady, shallow bursts as they navigated around sharp bends and over loose stones. She kept an eye on Layla, who was trailing slightly behind but moving with determined focus, and on Amir, who was scouting ahead, his gaze sharp and attentive.

Youssef, bringing up the rear, paused to check their surroundings every few steps. "Karim's men are tenacious," he murmured as they came to a temporary halt in a shaded alcove. "If they pick up our trail, we'll need to be ready to divert. This route is unpredictable, and we have to use that to our advantage."

Nadia checked the map fragment again, orienting herself by the landmarks around them. "If we can make it through the ridge pass, there's a hidden path leading up into the cliffs," she whispered, her eyes scanning the horizon. "It's risky, but it will give us a vantage point—and make it harder for Karim's men to track us."

The group nodded, steeling themselves as they prepared to press on. But just as they stepped back onto the narrow path, a faint shout echoed through the canyon, reverberating off the walls. The sound sent a chill down Ellie's spine, and she froze, listening as more voices followed, bouncing through the canyon like ghostly echoes.

"They're close," Amir muttered, his face tense. "We need to move. Now."

They picked up their pace, moving quickly but quietly along the path. The rough stones underfoot made each step treacherous, and Ellie focused on keeping her balance, her senses on high alert. The walls around them rose higher, narrowing as they ventured deeper into the canyon, creating a maze of winding trails and dead ends.

Just when they thought they'd put enough distance between themselves and Karim's men, the sharp crack of gunfire shattered the silence, echoing through the canyon like thunder. Ellie's heart raced as they dove behind a large boulder, pressing themselves against the cool stone. She could hear Layla's rapid breathing beside her, and Simon's steady grip on her shoulder, grounding her amidst the chaos.

"Stay low," Youssef hissed, motioning for them to keep down as another shot rang out, chipping the edge of the rock beside them. Dust and small stones showered over them, and Ellie stifled a cough, her pulse hammering.

Nadia glanced at the team, her eyes sharp with determination. "We need to split up," she said in a low voice. "If we move as a group, we'll be an easy target. We'll go in pairs and meet at the ridge pass."

Ellie and Simon exchanged a quick look, nodding in silent agreement. They would stick together, and with a quick gesture, Amir and Layla moved off to the left, while Youssef and Nadia took the right.

As Ellie and Simon broke off from the group, they kept close to the canyon wall, weaving between outcroppings and staying in the shadows. The sounds of Karim's men grew louder behind them, their voices sharp and frustrated as they searched for the team.

Ellie's breath came in quick, shallow bursts as she gripped Simon's hand, pulling him toward a narrow crevice hidden behind a cluster of boulders. They slipped inside, pressing themselves against the cool stone and holding their breaths as the sound of footsteps approached.

One of Karim's men came into view, his silhouette dark against the light filtering through the canyon. Ellie's heart pounded as he moved closer, his gaze sweeping the path, just inches from where they stood concealed in the shadows.

For a tense, agonizing moment, he seemed to hesitate, his gaze lingering on their hiding spot. Ellie tightened her grip on Simon's hand, bracing herself. But after a moment, the man turned, muttering in frustration as he moved down the path, his footsteps fading into the distance.

Ellie exhaled, feeling the tension drain from her muscles as she and Simon slipped back onto the path, their movements careful and quiet. They picked up their pace, weaving through the narrow passages with renewed urgency. The sound of voices faded, but Ellie knew they couldn't let their guard down—not yet.

As they reached a small clearing, they paused to catch their breath, scanning their surroundings. Simon's gaze shifted to a narrow path winding up the cliffside, and he pointed, his voice low. "If we take that route, we might get a vantage point over the canyon. It's risky, but it could give us the advantage."

Ellie nodded, following him as they scrambled up the path, using handholds carved by years of wind and erosion. The climb was steep, but the adrenaline coursing through her veins drove her forward. Finally, they reached a ledge, giving them a clear view of the canyon below.

From their vantage point, Ellie spotted the others moving along separate paths, their figures small against the vastness of the canyon. Karim's men were scattered, their movements erratic as they searched for the team. Ellie's heart raced as she saw a small group of men moving toward Amir and Layla's position, and she felt a surge of fear.

"Simon," she whispered urgently, pointing down to where the group was closing in on Amir and Layla. "They're heading right toward them."

Simon's face tightened, his gaze sharp as he assessed the situation. "We need a diversion," he said, his tone decisive. "Something to draw them away."

Without hesitation, Simon picked up a small stone and tossed it down the opposite side of the ledge, sending it clattering down the rocks. The sound echoed through the canyon, bouncing off the walls, and immediately drew the attention of Karim's men. They turned, their focus shifting to the noise, giving Amir and Layla the chance to slip further along their path undetected.

Ellie felt a wave of relief as she watched Amir and Layla move into the shadows, their figures disappearing from sight. She turned to Simon, gratitude and admiration filling her gaze. "Quick thinking," she whispered, giving his hand a grateful squeeze.

He smiled, brushing a strand of dust-streaked hair from her face. "We're in this together. No one gets left behind."

They moved along the ledge, using the height to their advantage as they made their way toward the ridge. The path was narrow, with sheer drops on either side, but Ellie kept her focus steady, trusting her instincts and Simon's guiding hand.

As they neared the ridge pass, the sound of footsteps echoed below them. Ellie glanced down, spotting two more of Karim's men moving along the base of the cliff, their eyes scanning the canyon floor. She stilled, watching as they passed beneath them, and waited until the men disappeared around a bend before she and Simon continued forward.

At last, they reached the ridge, where the rest of the team was waiting, their faces marked by exhaustion and relief. Layla's face lit up as she spotted Ellie and Simon, her eyes bright with gratitude.

"You made it," she breathed, her voice filled with relief. "I was worried..."

Ellie nodded, giving Layla's shoulder a reassuring squeeze. "We're all here. Now we just have to stay ahead of them."

Nadia unfolded the map fragment, her face resolute. "The hidden valley is just beyond this ridge. Once we're inside, we'll have more cover. But we need to move quickly."

Youssef nodded, his eyes scanning the landscape. "The desert isn't just an obstacle—it's our ally. We'll use it to keep us safe."

They set off together, navigating the rough terrain with renewed determination. Ellie felt a surge of energy as they moved deeper into the desert, the canyon walls giving way to open land, where sand dunes stretched out like waves frozen in time.

But just as they crested a dune, the unmistakable sound of engines roared to life behind them. Ellie's heart dropped as she saw a cloud of dust rising in the distance—Karim's men, relentless in their pursuit.

"We're not out of the woods yet," Amir muttered, his face tense.

Nadia looked around, her gaze sharp and calculating. "There's a narrow gorge just ahead. If we make it through, the sand will cover our tracks. We'll be harder to follow."

They moved with urgency, their footsteps kicking up sand as they descended into the gorge. The walls rose high around them, creating a natural maze that wound through the desert like a labyrinth. Ellie could feel her pulse racing, every nerve on edge as they navigated the twisting path, the roar of engines growing louder behind them.

Finally, they reached a fork in the gorge, and Nadia motioned for them to split up again, each group taking a different path to throw off their pursuers. Ellie and Simon took the left, their pace quick as they pressed on, feeling the shadows deepen around them.

The sound of engines faded, replaced by the quiet hush of the desert. As they reached a hidden alcove in the gorge, Ellie glanced over at Simon, her heart pounding but her spirit resolute.

They would find the treasure. They would protect it. And together, they would ensure that Karim's ruthless pursuit would end in failure.

AMIR'S SACRIFICE

The scorching afternoon sun cast long shadows over the narrow gorge as Ellie, Simon, and the rest of the team hurried through the winding passage, their footsteps muffled by the shifting sands beneath them. The sounds of Karim's men were still audible behind them, their relentless pursuit echoing off the canyon walls like a dark promise. Every twist and turn brought new tension, a constant reminder of the danger pressing in from all sides.

As they reached a fork in the path, Amir held up a hand, motioning for the group to stop. His sharp gaze surveyed the rocky terrain, assessing the best route forward. He looked to Nadia, his eyes filled with determination and urgency.

"Listen," Amir said in a low, steady voice, "we need a diversion if we're going to make it to the valley. Karim's men are too close. They know these canyons better than we realized."

Ellie's pulse quickened as she sensed the implication behind his words. "Amir, what are you suggesting?"

Amir gave her a reassuring smile, his expression calm. "I know these paths like the back of my hand. I can lead them on a false trail, give you enough time to make it to the valley. Once they're drawn away, I'll circle back and meet you."

Layla's face turned pale, her eyes wide with worry. "Amir, that's too risky. If they catch you—"

"They won't catch me," Amir interrupted gently, his voice filled with quiet confidence. "I know this land better than they do. I'll keep to the shadows, and with a little luck, I'll lead them far enough off course."

Nadia stepped forward, her eyes fierce with determination but laced with concern. "Amir, I can't ask you to do this. There must be another way."

He shook his head, placing a reassuring hand on her shoulder. "You're not asking, Nadia. I'm offering. I've always believed in this mission, in the purpose behind it. And I believe in all of you." His gaze softened, lingering on her for a moment longer than necessary. "This is my choice."

Ellie felt a lump form in her throat as she watched the silent exchange between Amir and Nadia. His loyalty to her was deeper than duty—it was a bond forged through years of trust, shared goals, and perhaps something more. She saw the unspoken words in their eyes, a silent understanding that spoke volumes.

Simon, his face somber, stepped forward. "Amir, are you sure? We can try another way..."

But Amir merely gave him a firm nod, a faint smile on his lips. "You'll all make it. That's what matters. Trust me, I'll be right behind you."

Before anyone could protest further, Amir moved swiftly, leading them down one of the paths until they reached a bend. He pointed to a faint trail on the opposite side of the gorge. "Take this path. It will lead you to the valley entrance."

He turned to go, but Nadia reached out, her hand closing over his arm. "Amir," she said, her voice trembling slightly, "please be careful."

Amir's smile softened, and he placed his hand over hers. "I promise, Nadia. I'll see you on the other side."

With a final nod to the group, Amir turned and sprinted back down the path, his silhouette disappearing into the shadowed gorge. The team watched him go, their hearts heavy with the weight of his sacrifice. Ellie felt a deep ache in her chest, a mixture of fear and admiration as Amir's figure grew smaller, swallowed by the shadows.

"Let's move," Simon urged quietly, his hand resting on Ellie's shoulder. "We need to honor his decision and make it to the valley."

They continued along the narrow path Amir had indicated, moving quickly but carefully, their footsteps silent as they wove through the winding canyons. Every step felt like a countdown, each second ticking by as they hoped against hope that Amir's diversion would buy them enough time.

As they neared the valley entrance, the distant sounds of shouting reached them, followed by another sharp crack of gunfire. Ellie's heart twisted as she thought of Amir, alone and facing Karim's men. She forced herself to focus, pushing down the fear that threatened to overwhelm her. Amir was clever, skilled, and knew this land better than anyone—if anyone could outsmart Karim's men, it was him.

Layla glanced back, her face stricken. "I can't believe he just... went back like that. He didn't even hesitate."

Nadia's voice was steady, though Ellie could see the tension in her clenched fists. "Amir has always been loyal to our mission. He believes in what we're doing, and he would do anything to protect this history."

The team pushed on, their spirits bolstered by Amir's sacrifice but tempered by a heavy sense of worry. They had almost reached the valley when they heard another round of gunfire, closer this time, the echoes bouncing off the canyon walls.

Ellie's heart clenched as the shots rang out, each one punctuating the silence like a countdown. Her thoughts were consumed with Amir, his brave face, his final smile, the way he'd looked at Nadia as if he'd already known what he would do. She forced herself to keep moving, reminding herself that Amir had made this choice for them.

As they rounded the final bend, the valley opened before them—a hidden expanse of rugged cliffs and twisted rock formations, dotted with patches of desert flora. The sky stretched wide above them, the blazing sun casting long shadows over the valley floor.

They hurried toward a sheltered area beneath a rocky overhang, catching their breath as they scanned the horizon. There was no sign of Karim's men, and Ellie felt a faint flicker of hope. Perhaps Amir's plan had worked, after all.

But then, just as they began to settle, a faint figure appeared on the ridge above them. Ellie squinted, her heart leaping as she recognized the outline of Amir, his hand raised in a signal. Relief flooded her, and she felt a grateful smile tug at her lips.

He'd made it.

But before she could react, another figure appeared behind him—one of Karim's men, his weapon raised. Ellie's heart froze, time seeming to slow as she watched the man take aim. She opened her mouth to shout, but the sound died in her throat, her mind racing as horror filled her.

Amir turned, his eyes widening as he spotted the man. Without hesitation, he moved, lunging toward his attacker. The two struggled, their figures locked in a desperate grapple on the edge of the ridge.

Nadia cried out, her voice a mixture of fear and desperation. "Amir!"

The gun fired, the sharp crack echoing across the valley. Ellie felt the world go silent, her breath catching as she watched Amir stumble, his form silhouetted against the bright sky. For a moment, he seemed to hover, suspended in time, his eyes meeting Nadia's across the distance.

Then, in a slow, terrible descent, Amir fell back, his body slipping over the edge of the ridge. Ellie's heart shattered as he disappeared from view, the finality of his sacrifice settling over the team like a dark cloud.

Nadia sank to her knees, her hand covering her mouth as she stared at the empty ridge, her face pale with shock and grief. Layla placed a hand on her shoulder, tears streaming down her face as the weight of Amir's loss settled over them.

Simon's hand tightened around Ellie's, his face etched with sorrow as he looked down at her. "He gave us a chance," he murmured, his voice choked with emotion. "Amir knew what he was doing. He made this choice to protect all of us."

Ellie nodded, though the grief in her chest felt like a physical ache. She looked back up at the ridge, her heart aching as she thought of Amir's courage, his loyalty, and the quiet, steadfast way he had supported them all.

Nadia stood slowly, her face hardened with resolve. She wiped her eyes, squaring her shoulders as she looked out over the valley. "Amir's sacrifice won't be in vain," she said, her voice steady despite the sorrow in her eyes. "We'll finish this. We'll protect the temple, the treasure, and everything he believed in."

Ellie reached out, placing a hand on Nadia's shoulder. "We'll honor him by seeing this mission through. For Amir."

The team gathered their things, their movements heavy but determined. Together, they turned toward the path leading deeper into the valley, each step carrying the weight of Amir's sacrifice and the knowledge that he had given his life to protect them.

As they moved deeper into the valley, Nadia stole one last glance back at the ridge, her heart aching. Though she'd witnessed Amir's fall, something inside her resisted believing he was truly gone. It was as if a small, stubborn spark of hope clung to her, refusing to extinguish.

Ellie placed a comforting hand on her shoulder. "Nadia, I know he meant the world to you."

Nadia nodded, swallowing hard. "He... he did. And I'll honor him by finishing what he started."

They continued through the valley, each step heavy with the weight of Amir's loss. But in the quiet moments, when the desert winds whispered around them, Nadia couldn't shake the feeling that this might not be the last time she would see him.

CHAPTER

23

A HIDDEN CHAMBER

The low sun cast deep shadows across the valley as Ellie, Simon, Nadia, Layla, and Youssef moved toward the cliffside. Following Amir's directions and the ancient map, they found themselves in front of a towering rock face covered with faint carvings. Each symbol was as ancient as the land itself, mirroring the mysterious markings they'd uncovered in the original temple.

"This is it," Ellie whispered, awe filling her voice as she recognized the carvings. "It matches the map perfectly."

Nadia studied the markings closely, her fingers tracing the weathered stone with reverence. "If we can find a hidden entrance... it should lead us to the chamber."

They searched the rock face in silence, each one acutely aware of the potential treasure hidden within. Just as the excitement began to give way to frustration, Simon's hand brushed over a section of stone that felt slightly different, as though worn down by use. He pressed it, and with a low rumble, a narrow passage opened before them, revealing a hidden way into the cliff.

The group exchanged awed glances, then filed into the passage, their flashlights illuminating the ancient stone walls covered in constellations, intricate symbols, and celestial figures. The air was thick and cool, carrying the earthy scent of stone untouched for centuries.

At last, the passage opened into a vast, hidden chamber. The ceiling arched high above them, lost in shadow, while rows of pedestals and towering statues filled the space. Each pedestal held carefully crafted artifacts—relics of a civilization that had remained hidden from the world for centuries.

Layla let out a soft gasp as she took in the grandeur of the chamber. "This... it's beyond anything we've ever seen."

Ellie scanned the pedestals, her heart racing as she recognized some of the artifacts. They mirrored those they had found earlier in their dig—small, polished figures, intricate amulets, and delicate silver discs etched with celestial symbols. One disc in particular caught her eye. She stepped closer, her pulse quickening as she noted its resemblance to the one they'd already unearthed.

"This disc," Ellie murmured, her hand hovering over it. "It's identical to the one we found earlier. There must be some connection."

Nadia nodded, her face filled with excitement. "It could be a key—something that unites the artifacts we've found. If we compare the two, we may be able to unlock the full message or purpose behind them."

Layla's fingers brushed over a delicate silver amulet nearby, her eyes wide with wonder. "This culture clearly valued these objects. Each one is crafted with precision and care—it's almost as if they were part of a ritual, or a way of communing with the stars."

Simon took several photographs of the scene, capturing the arrangement and details of the artifacts for later study. They understood that taking too many items would disturb the integrity of the site and risk attracting unwanted attention, but the silver disc, along with one or two smaller items, seemed essential.

As they carefully packed the disc and the amulet, Layla's excitement gave way to a growing unease. She glanced around the chamber, feeling a chill as the shadows deepened. "Does anyone else feel like we're being watched?"

Ellie looked over at her, feeling a similar prickling sensation down her spine. She scanned the statues lining the chamber walls, their shadowed faces appearing almost lifelike in the dim light. The ancient carvings on the walls seemed to pulse with an energy all their own, as if the very stone carried the memories of the people who had worshipped here.

"It is a sacred space," Nadia murmured, her gaze reverent. "But we're here to honor it, not to disturb it. Whatever spirits remain, they'll see that."

They continued documenting the artifacts and carvings in silence, each of them aware that their presence in the chamber was temporary. The sense of reverence hung heavily over them, tempered by Layla's lingering feeling of unease.

As they turned to leave, Layla lingered at the central altar, her gaze drawn to an amulet that matched one of the artifacts they'd discovered weeks ago. She traced her fingers over its surface, noticing an inscription in the same mysterious language as the disc.

"This inscription..." she whispered. "It's almost as if it's connected to a prayer, or a plea. Like a message to the gods."

But before she could examine it further, the distant echo of footsteps reached them from the passageway. Ellie's heart skipped a beat, the sound snapping her out of her reverie. They exchanged alarmed glances, realizing Karim's men had somehow managed to follow their trail.

"We need to get out of here, now," Simon whispered urgently. "If Karim's men find us here, we'll have no way of escaping."

They gathered their few chosen items, moving swiftly toward the entrance. Nadia, her face steeled with determination, gestured for the group to stay close as they navigated the narrow passage, doing their best to keep silent. They knew Karim's men wouldn't destroy the artifacts—they would see the chamber's treasures as valuable assets for the black market. But they were ruthless and wouldn't hesitate to use force to get what they wanted.

As they neared the exit, Layla felt a twinge of hesitation, a feeling that something—someone—was watching her. She cast a glance back, her heart racing as she thought she saw movement in the shadows. A faint silhouette, just out of reach of the flashlight's beam, seemed to linger near the altar. Her breath caught, the hairs on her arms standing on end.

But Simon reached for her hand, pulling her forward. "Come on, Layla. We need to go."

Reluctantly, she let him lead her out of the chamber, though the image of that shadow stayed with her, unsettling her even as they emerged into the open air.

Outside, the sky had darkened further, the cliffs casting long shadows over the valley. The team kept low as they moved along the rock walls, their footsteps silent against the sand. Behind them, the muffled voices of Karim's men echoed from within the chamber, laced with greedy excitement as they uncovered the artifacts.

Nadia glanced back, a fierce look of resolve on her face. "They may have found the chamber, but they won't find everything. We have the disc and our notes—they'll never know the true purpose of the temple."

Ellie nodded, her gaze steely as she looked at the treasures they carried, a testament to the lives and beliefs of an ancient people. "We'll protect this history, no matter the cost."

As they moved quickly along the valley path, Ellie spotted something on the ground—a glint of metal half-buried in the sand. She picked it up, her pulse quickening as she recognized it: a worn button from a jacket, scuffed and dusty but familiar.

It was the same as the one Amir had been wearing.

Ellie tucked the button into her pocket, glancing at Nadia. She kept silent for now, not wanting to raise hopes without proof. But as they made their way toward the safety of the next canyon, a small spark of hope took root within her.

Perhaps Amir wasn't truly gone. Perhaps, somewhere in this vast desert, he was still watching over them.

THE FINAL STAND

The team had barely caught their breath as they emerged from the narrow canyon path into a small, open clearing. The shadows of the towering cliffs stretched long and dark over the desert floor, the sun dipping low on the horizon and casting a fiery glow. A warm breeze swept through, stirring up clouds of dust and sand that hung thick in the air.

They were exhausted, still reeling from the discovery in the hidden chamber and the narrow escape from Karim's men. Ellie glanced at her teammates, their faces etched with tension but filled with a steely resolve. She tightened her grip on her pack, where the silver disc and the few carefully chosen relics were tucked safely inside. The knowledge that these artifacts represented pieces of a lost history weighed on her, but so did the memory of Amir's sacrifice and the promise she felt to see this mission through.

Beside her, Simon placed a reassuring hand on her shoulder. She could feel the strength in his touch, his silent support calming her nerves as they pressed onward. Together, they led the team through the clearing, searching for a path that would lead them to safety.

As they pressed on, a sudden, harsh voice cut through the desert stillness. "I wouldn't take another step if I were you."

Ellie's heart froze. She whipped around to see Karim and a group of his men stepping out from the shadows. Their expressions were dark and predatory, eyes gleaming with greed and triumph. Karim stood at the forefront, his gaze fixed intently on Ellie and the team, a cold smile spreading across his face.

Simon stiffened beside her, his jaw clenching as he recognized Karim's unmistakable silhouette. Ellie felt her own fear harden into resolve, a fierce protectiveness rising within her. She glanced around, noticing the absence of Youssef, who had quietly slipped away earlier. They had assumed he'd gone ahead to secure their next path, but his disappearance only added to her sense of vulnerability.

"You thought you could just walk away with those relics?" Karim's voice dripped with mockery, his tone calm but filled with a quiet menace. He held a flashlight in one hand, its beam flicking between the team members, who stood rooted to the spot.

Ellie's heart raced, but she squared her shoulders, stepping protectively in front of Layla and meeting Karim's gaze with unflinching resolve. "These artifacts don't belong to you, Karim," she said, her voice steady. "They belong to history, to the people who created them. And I'll be damned if I let you take them."

Karim's eyes narrowed, and he took a step closer, his expression darkening. "Such a brave speech, Dr. Whitcombe. But I'm afraid you're in no position to make demands." He raised his hand, and one of his men revealed a lighter, holding it dangerously close to a bundle of parchment and photos they'd managed to seize from the site.

Ellie's breath hitched as she recognized their carefully documented notes and photographs—the irreplaceable evidence of their findings. Her mind raced, assessing the situation, trying to determine if they had any chance of escape.

"Turn over what you've taken from the site," Karim said, his voice dripping with impatience. "Hand me the disc, and all of the relics, or this documentation—everything you've worked so hard to record—goes up in flames."

Simon moved slightly closer to Ellie, his eyes flashing with anger. "You have no right, Karim. You're a thief—a coward who preys on history for his own profit."

Karim's smile tightened, his eyes gleaming with malice. "Profit, honor—it's all the same. The difference is, I'm not weighed down by your romantic ideals. History is valuable, and I intend to make the most of it. But if you want to cling to those ideals, then you'll have to watch as I burn every last piece of it."

Ellie's pulse thundered in her ears as she watched Karim hold their precious work hostage. She felt anger rising within her, fierce and unyielding, a protective fury that pushed back against her fear. These were her friends, her team, her family in this relentless desert, and she would protect them—and their discoveries—no matter the cost.

"You're not taking a thing, Karim," Ellie said, her voice firm and filled with defiance. "If you think we'll hand anything over to you, you're sorely mistaken."

Karim raised an eyebrow, clearly taken aback by her resolve. But then he chuckled, a low, mocking sound that sent a chill down her spine. "Oh, I think you'll reconsider, Dr. Whitcombe. After all, I have more men, more weapons, and you're in the middle of nowhere."

Simon shifted, positioning himself between Ellie and Karim, his voice low but fierce. "If you try to take anything from us, you'll have to go through me."

But Ellie didn't waver. She took a step forward, her eyes blazing with an intensity that surprised even her. "You have no idea what we're capable of, Karim. We've crossed deserts, survived threats, and endured sacrifices you can't even imagine. These relics mean more to us than you could ever comprehend, and if you think you can intimidate us into giving up, you're in for a rude awakening."

The team shifted subtly, drawing closer to each other, united in their stance. Nadia, Layla, and Simon moved forward, each one ready to face whatever Karim would throw at them. Ellie could feel the strength of their resolve, an unspoken promise that they wouldn't back down.

Karim's smile faded, replaced by a glint of frustration and anger. "Very well," he said, his voice dripping with contempt. "If you won't hand over the relics, then I'll take them from you by force."

With a sharp gesture, Karim motioned to his men, who began advancing, their expressions ruthless and intent. Ellie's breath caught, and she instinctively moved to shield Layla, her eyes scanning their surroundings for any potential escape route. But the cliff walls were high, and the only path was blocked by Karim's men.

Just as she prepared to fight back, a loud whistle echoed from the cliffs above. The sound was sharp and clear, cutting through the tension like a blade. Karim and his men froze, their heads snapping up toward the source of the sound.

Ellie's heart skipped a beat as she looked up, catching sight of a lone figure silhouetted against the sunset—a tall, lean man with familiar features. Her breath caught as hope and disbelief flooded her chest. It was Amir.

He stood on the ledge above them, his face shadowed but unmistakably alive, his stance strong and unwavering. Ellie felt a surge of relief and joy, the sight of him rekindling her hope. He was alive, and he had come back for them.

Amir's voice echoed down the cliff, firm and unyielding. "Karim, you're outnumbered, and outmatched. If you want to take these artifacts, you'll have to go through me first."

Karim's face twisted in surprise, then fury, as he took in the sight of Amir. "So, the deserter returns," he sneered. "You're a fool if you think you can take on all of us."

Amir smirked, his eyes flashing with defiance. "I've faced worse odds than you, Karim. And I won't let you desecrate this site or steal its history."

At that moment, two Ministry guards appeared beside Amir, each carrying a weapon aimed squarely at Karim and his men. The tables had turned, and Karim's men hesitated, glancing at each other with uncertainty as they realized they were no longer in control.

Ellie took advantage of the shift, stepping forward with newfound confidence. "It's over, Karim. This land and its history belong to the people who respect it, not to vultures like you."

Karim's gaze darted between Ellie, Amir, and the armed guards above. His jaw clenched, and for a moment, Ellie thought he might try to fight. But then he lowered his hand, his expression bitter as he motioned to his men.

"Fall back," he snarled, his voice filled with rage. "This isn't over, Whitcombe. You've made an enemy today."

Ellie held his gaze, her chin raised defiantly. "I'll sleep just fine knowing that, Karim. We'll protect this history from people like you."

With a final glare, Karim and his men retreated, disappearing into the shadows of the canyon. Ellie felt a weight lift from her chest, and she let out a long, shaky breath as the tension drained from her body.

Amir climbed down from the ledge, a faint smile on his face as he approached the group. Ellie met him with wide eyes, her heart swelling with gratitude and disbelief. "Amir... we thought you—"

Amir's gaze softened, and he gave her a small nod. "It'll take more than Karim to keep me down. I told you I'd meet you on the other side."

Nadia stepped forward, her eyes shining with unshed tears as she looked at him. "Amir, you... you saved us."

He gave her a gentle smile, his voice soft. "I told you—this mission matters. To all of us."

As the team gathered around him, Ellie felt a surge of pride and relief. They had faced Karim's threat and emerged stronger, united in their purpose. And with Amir by their side once again, they were ready to finish what they had started.

Under the desert's fading light, Ellie knew they would honor this history, preserve its secrets, and stand together against anyone who tried to destroy it.

25

YOUSSEF'S RESCUE

The quiet desert night settled around them as the team regrouped, the adrenaline from their encounter with Karim slowly ebbing away. Ellie felt the weight of exhaustion pressing on her, but the relief of Amir's return kept her spirits high. She looked around at her friends—Simon, Nadia, Amir, and Layla—and felt a surge of gratitude. They had faced down a dangerous man and stood together, stronger than ever.

Just as the tension seemed to be dissipating, the distant sound of engines rumbled through the canyon. The team froze, instinctively bracing themselves as the headlights of several vehicles appeared in the distance, cutting through the darkness.

"Stay alert," Simon murmured, his gaze fixed on the approaching convoy. "This might not be over."

But as the vehicles drew closer, Ellie recognized the lead truck—a familiar battered vehicle belonging to none other than Youssef. Relief washed over her as she spotted his silhouette in the driver's seat, flanked by a convoy of police vehicles from Jordan's national law enforcement.

Youssef brought his truck to a stop just a few meters away and jumped out, a grin spreading across his face. Behind him, armed officers stepped out of their vehicles, moving with precision and purpose as they surrounded the team. Ellie and the others exchanged surprised glances, realizing that this was no ordinary escort—this was a full police operation.

"Youssef!" Ellie exclaimed, her voice filled with gratitude and relief as he approached. "We thought you'd disappeared!"

Youssef chuckled, nodding toward the officers around them. "Had a little business to take care of. Karim's not just a small-time smuggler—he's got his hands in some very dark dealings, and I knew he wouldn't go down without a fight. So I brought a few friends to help ensure his... departure."

Nadia stared at the officers with wide eyes, her expression a mixture of shock and admiration. "You... you brought the police?"

Youssef's grin widened. "I knew Karim had been on their radar for a while. He's been smuggling artifacts and bribing officials for years, but his web is vast. When I realized he was here, I made a few calls. The police were more than happy to join forces with us and make sure Karim can't escape again."

An officer stepped forward, his expression respectful as he nodded to the team. "Dr. Whitcombe, Dr. al-Masri, my name is Officer Samir Haddad," he said with a steady gaze. "My team and I have been tracking Karim's activities for some time. We were close to bringing him down, but his connections run deep. Thanks to your group and Youssef's tip, we now have the evidence we need to make his arrest indisputable."

Ellie felt a swell of pride as the officer continued, his gaze shifting to Youssef. "Youssef has been a critical ally in this operation, coordinating with us to catch Karim in the act. His arrest today is the culmination of a long investigation, one that now has irrefutable evidence of his crimes, thanks in part to you."

Ellie's heart pounded with relief as she realized that Karim's days of evading justice were truly over. As if on cue, two officers approached, leading Karim in handcuffs. His face was a mask of anger and desperation, his defiant gaze fixed on Ellie and her team as he was marched forward.

"You think this is over?" Karim spat, his voice filled with venom. "You think I won't be back?"

Officer Haddad beside him tightened his grip, his voice calm but firm. "Enough, Karim. You're facing serious charges—smuggling, bribery, artifact trafficking. This is the end of the line."

Karim's scowl deepened, but as he took in the solemn faces of the officers surrounding him, the defiance drained from his expression. In one last, desperate attempt, he looked toward the lead officer. "I have information," he said quickly. "Contacts in high places. I can help you take down others in the network if you let me go."

Officer Haddad's face remained impassive. "We already have an extensive dossier on your activities, Karim, as well as a record of your contacts. The Ministry of Antiquities and the government have authorized a full investigation into your operations. We won't need your help."

Amir crossed his arms, watching Karim with a small smile of satisfaction. "It's over, Karim. You exploited this land, stole its history, and tried to profit from it. You won't get the chance to do that again."

With a final scowl, Karim was led away, his footsteps fading into the quiet of the desert night. Ellie felt a weight lift from her shoulders, a sense of justice and closure settling over her. She looked to Youssef, gratitude shining in her eyes. "Youssef, we owe you so much. We were at a dead end, and you came through for us."

He shrugged, his expression modest but pleased. "I'm just glad to help protect what matters. This land's history is sacred, and it belongs to everyone who respects it."

Simon clapped Youssef on the shoulder, his voice filled with admiration. "You're a hero, Youssef. Truly."

Officer Haddid approached, handing a sealed document stamped with the official insignia of Jordan's Ministry of Antiquities. He bowed respectfully as he addressed the team. "The Ministry extends its gratitude for your dedication and courage. You've safeguarded a priceless part of Jordan's heritage."

Nadia opened the document, her face lighting up as she read it aloud. "The Ministry is offering us special access to a future excavation," she said, her voice filled with wonder. "In Petra—beneath the Treasury. They're inviting us to join their team."

Ellie's heart raced with excitement at the mention of Petra, one of Jordan's most revered sites. Access to the area beneath the Treasury was a rare privilege, one granted only to the most trusted archaeologists.

"This is an incredible honor," she whispered, her voice filled with awe. "To have a role in such a significant excavation..."

Amir's eyes shone with pride as he looked at Nadia. "Your dedication brought us here, Nadia. This invitation is a testament to everything you've achieved."

Nadia smiled, her cheeks flushed with pride. "This invitation belongs to all of us. We've worked together, protected each other, and preserved history. And we're just getting started."

Officer Haddid nodded solemnly. "The government of Jordan is deeply grateful for your efforts. Because of you, Karim's network will face justice, and our heritage remains protected."

As the officers prepared to depart, Youssef looked out over the quiet desert, his expression thoughtful. "I may not be an archaeologist, but I've always believed in protecting the past. Working with all of you has been an honor."

Ellie stepped forward, placing a hand on Youssef's shoulder. "You're part of this mission, Youssef, as much as any of us. We couldn't have done it without you."

As the police convoy headed back toward the city with Karim and his men in custody, the team gathered around Youssef, reflecting on all they had accomplished together. They had come as strangers, brought together by a shared purpose, but they were leaving as family.

Under the desert's vast, starlit sky, Ellie looked around at her friends, feeling a deep sense of pride and gratitude. They had faced danger, betrayal, and the weight of history, but they had protected something priceless. And now, with the promise of a future excavation in Petra, their journey was far from over.

Simon slipped his arm around her shoulders, his voice filled with warmth. "We did it, Ellie. We kept history safe, together."

Ellie leaned against him, smiling as she looked out at the desert. "And we'll keep doing it, Simon. There's so much left to uncover."

With renewed purpose and a bond stronger than ever, the team turned their faces toward the desert, ready for whatever lay ahead.

26

RECLAIMING THE ARTIFACTS

The desert lay quiet and still as the team returned to the excavation site. The vast, open landscape seemed to echo their footsteps, the tension of recent days softened in the quiet expanse around them. Ellie took a deep breath, feeling the coolness of the morning air and letting it calm her racing thoughts. The site was now free from the chaos and threats they'd faced, and for the first time in days, she felt a sense of peace settle over her.

With Karim and his men in police custody, the team had official permission to recover the artifacts they'd uncovered, ensuring they would be transferred to Jordan's National Museum. This was not only a victory over Karim's greed but a promise fulfilled to the ancient guardians who had watched over this site for centuries.

As the team gathered the artifacts, now meticulously cataloged and wrapped in protective layers, each member worked in silence, acutely aware of the history contained within each relic. From the delicate silver disc to the amulets and carved figurines, each item spoke of a culture that had been hidden away, protected by the sands of time.

Layla carefully handled a small stone figurine, her fingers tracing its intricate details. "These are so much more than just objects," she murmured, almost to herself. "They're fragments of lives and beliefs, each carrying a story we'll never fully understand."

Ellie nodded, sharing Layla's deep sense of respect. "And now, they're in our care. It's our responsibility to ensure these stories aren't just preserved but honored. They belong to Jordan and to the people who value their heritage."

Nadia's gaze was filled with pride as she looked at the carefully arranged artifacts. "The Ministry of Antiquities has agreed to house these relics in a dedicated wing at the museum, open to scholars and the public. They'll stay in Jordan, where they belong, and the knowledge we've uncovered will be accessible to those who seek it."

Youssef arrived with Ministry officials in tow, his expression one of quiet satisfaction. He approached Ellie and the team with a respectful nod. "These officials will oversee the transport and placement of the artifacts. Jordan's people will now have access to their history, thanks to your efforts."

One of the Ministry officials, a dignified woman named Hana, stepped forward, her expression warm. "We deeply appreciate your dedication. Artifacts of this magnitude require a delicate balance of preservation and accessibility. You've shown respect for our culture, and we thank you for that."

Amir, who had been organizing their notes and photographs, glanced up, his voice filled with pride. "This mission wasn't just about discovery; it was about protection. Each artifact here tells a story that deserves to be told, and it's reassuring to know that it will be."

Simon finished securing the last of their documents and photographs, a deep sense of accomplishment in his expression. "We were lucky to find these artifacts intact. The knowledge they contain—the beliefs, the stories... it's a part of humanity that could have been lost forever."

Layla glanced at the silver disc, carefully examining the delicate etchings, which matched the one they'd previously found in the temple. Tilting it toward the light, she watched as the symbols reflected faintly. "These symbols, these carvings—they connect everything we've seen. It's as though the people who crafted these items intended for future generations to uncover something profound."

Nadia nodded thoughtfully, her gaze lingering on the disc. "If we're right, these artifacts are part of a larger legacy. The symbols and patterns form a language, perhaps even a guide, speaking to us across time."

As the team documented each item for the museum's records, Hana approached Nadia, her voice filled with admiration. "You and your team have protected our heritage in the truest sense. Jordan thanks you all deeply."

Nadia inclined her head, her expression proud but humble. "It was our privilege. This history, this culture... it belongs to Jordan, and it's our honor to be a part of preserving it."

Amir joined the conversation, his tone both respectful and resolute. "The fight to protect these artifacts was worth it. They represent more than history—they're a part of the lives and beliefs of those who came before us. They deserve to be safe."

As the last of the items were wrapped and secured, the team watched as Ministry officials loaded them with utmost care, setting them on a course toward the museum where they would be cataloged and displayed for the public. Ellie felt a deep sense of satisfaction as she watched each item safely packed away, knowing that the people of Jordan would soon have the chance to see and learn from these treasures.

Youssef nodded toward Ellie, a small smile playing on his lips. "Your efforts here won't be forgotten. The people of Jordan have a part of their heritage back, thanks to you."

Ellie returned his smile, feeling the weight of his words settle over her. This mission had changed them all, grounding them in a purpose that went beyond their professional callings. They had become guardians, bound to the stories and people of Jordan in a way that was both humbling and profound.

As the sun rose higher in the sky, casting golden light across the desert, the team turned to leave the site, their work complete. There was no fanfare, no applause—only the quiet satisfaction of a mission accomplished, of history protected for those who would come after.

Ellie looked around at her friends, each of them reflecting on the importance of the artifacts they'd reclaimed. This place, these relics, had become a part of them, shaping their understanding and respect for a culture that had been nearly lost to time.

They knew they would soon leave Jordan, but they would do so knowing that they had made a difference. And as they walked back toward the vehicles waiting to take them back to the city, Ellie felt a quiet pride in what they had achieved together.

The desert's ancient guardians could rest easy once more, knowing that their stories, their legacies, were safe.

A FAREWELL WITH THE DOCTORS

The morning was quiet as Ellie and Simon walked through the arched entrance of the university's stone courtyard, their footsteps echoing softly against the centuries-old walls. Though the warm desert air carried the familiar sounds of Amman's busy streets, the university grounds felt like a haven, as though they were stepping into a timeless sanctuary.

Waiting for them beneath the shade of a large olive tree stood Dr. Khalid Abbas and Professor Malik Ibrahim, two figures who had become guides, mentors, and friends in their journey through Jordan's ancient history. Their eyes lit up as they saw Ellie and Simon approaching, each of them carrying the weight of the years with quiet dignity.

As Ellie and Simon neared, Professor Malik extended a warm hand, his smile broad and genuine. "You have done great things here, my friends," he said, his deep voice filled with admiration. "Jordan owes you a debt of gratitude."

Dr. Abbas inclined his head in agreement. "Your journey has not only honored this land's history but has also inspired those of us who work to preserve it. You remind us that dedication to cultural preservation requires both courage and humility."

Ellie smiled, her heart swelling with gratitude as she took their hands in turn. "It's hard to believe this journey is coming to an end," she said, glancing at Simon, who nodded in agreement. "We've learned so much, and the guidance you've both given us... it's hard to put into words how deeply it's impacted us."

"Ellie," Malik said, his gaze warm but stern. "I think, after all we've been through, it's time you call me by my first name. 'Professor Malik' makes me sound too distinguished for someone who's trudged through the desert dust."

Dr. Abbas gave a nod of agreement, a twinkle in his eye. "And you must call me Khalid. We are no longer just colleagues; we are friends. Titles have no place among friends."

Ellie's smile deepened, feeling the warmth of their acceptance. "Khalid, Malik—it's an honor."

They all settled on a bench under the tree, each relishing the chance to pause and reflect after so many days of intensity and excitement. Ellie looked at Malik, remembering the first time they'd met, his scholarly gaze and calm authority offering reassurance and insight.

"Malik," she began, "your knowledge of Jordan's history has been like a thread connecting us to each discovery we made. It was as though we were never alone in the desert, because your teachings were always with us."

Malik gave a humble nod, his eyes crinkling at the corners as he listened. "Ah, Ellie, history isn't just a story to be told. It is a way of understanding ourselves and our responsibilities. Those who came before us left us lessons in the sands, in the stones, in the whispers of the wind. It is up to us to protect those lessons and to honor them."

He looked at Simon, his gaze penetrating. "You both have taken that responsibility to heart, and it is no small thing. You could have simply written about your journey or moved on to other pursuits, but you stayed. You fought for this history because you felt its weight. This is the spirit of true stewardship."

Simon took a deep breath, nodding thoughtfully. "Before this trip, I thought of archaeology as exploration and discovery. I saw it as a way to uncover secrets of the past. But now, I realize it's also about respect and care. It's about protecting what's been left behind, not for ourselves, but for those who will come after us."

Khalid looked at Simon with a warm smile, the wisdom in his eyes undeniable. "Exactly, Simon. True preservation requires empathy—a sense of connection with the people who created these relics and artifacts, and a desire to see their voices continue to be heard. The past is never just gone. It lives on in the memories we preserve."

Ellie felt a lump in her throat as she listened to Khalid. She had come to Jordan seeking adventure, a chance to immerse herself in a new place and a new story, but what she had found was something much greater—a profound respect for the people, the land, and the stories they shared.

"Khalid," she said softly, "I hope that Simon and I can bring even a fraction of the passion you've shown us back home. You've taught us what it means to be guardians of history, to protect a legacy that's bigger than any one of us."

Khalid's smile was gentle. "You already carry that passion within you, Ellie. I saw it in both of you from the moment we met. And Jordan has been enriched by your presence here, just as you have been shaped by your experiences in our country."

Malik's gaze grew thoughtful as he regarded them both. "What you carry now, Ellie and Simon, is more than knowledge. It's a sense of place, a respect for heritage, and a commitment to ensuring that the stories of the past are never silenced. As you return home, hold onto that. Let it guide you in whatever you choose to do next."

Ellie nodded, feeling a deep connection to these men who had opened her eyes to a world she had barely begun to understand. "It's strange," she said, glancing around at the familiar stone walls and sunlit trees. "I feel like I'm leaving home all over again."

Khalid reached out, placing a comforting hand on her shoulder. "That is how the desert works. Once it has touched you, it will always be a part of you. But know this—you are always welcome here, Ellie, Simon. Our doors are open, and the sands will remember you."

The words brought an ache to Ellie's heart, but it was a good ache—a feeling of belonging, of being part of something far greater than herself. She looked at Simon, who gave her a gentle nod, understanding the depth of her emotions. This journey had not just been an adventure; it had been a calling.

Malik glanced at Khalid, and the two men exchanged a silent look, as though communicating something only they could fully grasp. Turning back to the Whitcombes, Malik spoke, his voice steady and filled with purpose. "There is one more lesson we would like to leave you with, if you'll allow it."

Ellie and Simon nodded eagerly, leaning in, ready to soak in whatever wisdom their mentors would impart.

"Remember that preservation is not just about protecting physical artifacts," Malik said. "It's about protecting identity. History, culture, beliefs—these are the core of who we are. Every object you touch, every story you tell, is part of a much larger tapestry. And as caretakers of history, we must remember to approach our work with humility and a respect for the culture we are preserving."

Khalid continued, his voice gentle but firm. "When we encounter the past, we must never assume we understand everything about it. History is full of mysteries, and some of them are meant to remain mysteries. Approach your work with curiosity, yes, but also with reverence for what cannot be fully known."

The two men paused, their words sinking in, and Ellie felt a sense of awe at the depth of their wisdom. She looked at Simon, seeing the same reflection of understanding and respect in his eyes. These were lessons they would carry for a lifetime, words that would guide them through their future endeavors.

"Thank you," Ellie whispered, her voice thick with emotion. "For everything."

Khalid and Malik each extended their hands, and Ellie and Simon shook them, feeling the weight of their respect and gratitude in the firm grip of their mentors. It was more than a farewell; it was a passing of the torch, a recognition that Ellie and Simon would carry forward what they had learned, weaving it into their lives and their work.

Malik's eyes softened as he watched them. "This is not goodbye, Ellie and Simon. It is simply, 'Until we meet again.' You will always have a place here, and we will be waiting to hear of your future discoveries."

As they prepared to leave, Ellie took one last look at the courtyard, the sunlight filtering through the leaves, casting dappled shadows on the ancient stone. She felt as though she were taking a piece of this place with her, carrying it in her heart as a reminder of the wisdom she had gained and the friendships she had forged.

Khalid and Malik watched as they turned to go, their eyes reflecting a quiet pride and the satisfaction of seeing two of their students embrace the path of true stewardship.

And as Ellie and Simon walked away from the courtyard, hand in hand, they knew that the lessons they had learned here would guide them through whatever lay ahead. They were leaving Jordan, but they were taking with them a part of its heart and spirit—lessons from the desert, wisdom from their mentors, and a promise to protect the past for the generations to come.

28

GOODBYES AND NEW BEGINNINGS

The morning sun cast a warm glow over the small airport terminal as the Whitcombes gathered with their friends for the last time. Each goodbye felt like the end of a chapter, and Ellie felt her heart grow heavier with each passing moment. This had been a journey of a lifetime, and the friends standing beside her had become family, sharing not only their professional mission but their dreams, fears, and memories.

Nadia stood close, her eyes reflecting both pride and sadness as she reached out to clasp Ellie's hands. "It's hard to let you go, Ellie," she said, her voice soft. "You and Simon have become a part of us—part of this mission."

Ellie squeezed her hands, feeling the warmth and strength in her friend's touch. "Nadia, I can't thank you enough. You welcomed us into your world and taught us so much about history, dedication, and courage. Jordan... this place, these people... it will always feel like a second home to us because of you."

Nadia smiled, blinking back tears. Then, with a hesitant glance around, she pulled Ellie into a warm hug, whispering, "Take care of yourself, Ellie. This journey wouldn't have been the same without you."

Ellie hugged her tightly, sensing that the gesture, though rare, expressed the deep bond they had forged. As they broke apart, Simon stepped forward, shaking Nadia's hand and offering her a grateful nod. "Thank you, Nadia," he said, his voice thick with emotion. "For everything. We look forward to hearing about all the amazing discoveries you and your team will make."

Amir approached next, his eyes shining with pride. "You two brought a spirit to this mission that inspired us all," he said, a mischievous smile breaking through. "And you survived our infamous desert! Not many can say that." He chuckled, and Ellie laughed with him, remembering their long days trekking through sand and sun.

"Amir," Ellie said, her tone playful but sincere, "I think you saved our lives more times than I can count. Your bravery and resourcefulness kept us going. We couldn't have done this without you."

Amir's expression softened, and he gave her a respectful nod. "I was glad to be a part of it. And I'll keep an eye on things here—you'll always have someone watching over Jordan's treasures."

Then, defying convention, Amir opened his arms and enveloped Ellie in a heartfelt embrace, patting her on the back. Simon joined them, sharing a quick handshake with Amir that turned into a half-hug, a show of brotherly affection.

Layla stepped forward, her eyes wide with emotion as she looked at Ellie and Simon, her mentors and friends. "You've shown me what it truly means to protect history," she said, her voice barely above a whisper. "I always knew I wanted to be an archaeologist, but now... now I know that I want to fight for our heritage. For the things that matter."

Ellie felt a surge of pride as she listened to Layla's words. She reached out, pulling her close in an affectionate hug. "You have everything you need, Layla. You're passionate, strong, and smart. Jordan's history couldn't be in better hands."

Layla's eyes shone as she stepped back, smiling at both Ellie and Simon. "Promise me you'll stay in touch. I'll be waiting for news from you, and I'll keep you updated on everything we're working on here."

"We wouldn't have it any other way," Simon replied, grinning. "You're family now, Layla."

As Ellie and Simon shared parting words with Nadia, she turned and gestured to two familiar figures approaching from the entrance: Amina, with her warm smile and caring eyes, and Rafiq, standing tall and watchful as ever. Ellie's face lit up as she saw them.

"Amina! Rafiq!" Ellie exclaimed, hurrying over to greet them. She felt a rush of gratitude as she took in the two who had sheltered and supported them when they needed it most.

Amina pulled Ellie into a warm embrace, her voice soft. "Ellie, you and Simon have been like family. We'll miss you both, but please know you're always welcome here."

Ellie's eyes shimmered as she hugged Amina tightly. "You made us feel at home from the very beginning. Thank you, Amina, for everything."

Rafiq stepped forward, his usual serious demeanor softened by a small smile. "It was an honor to protect you and your team," he said, giving a respectful nod to Simon as well. "You all came here to protect our history, and for that, you will always have a place with us."

Simon extended his hand, and Rafiq shook it firmly. "We couldn't have done this without you, Rafiq," Simon said. "Your support kept us safe, and your home was a sanctuary."

Then, as if on cue, Youssef approached, his familiar, kind eyes meeting Ellie's with a warmth that reflected years of loyalty. "So, this is it," he said with a quiet smile. "I never thought the simple task of taxiing would lead to this—a lifetime of memories."

Ellie's heart swelled as she looked at him. "Youssef, you didn't just taxi us around. You introduced us to Rafiq, stood by us when things were uncertain, and—above all—you saved us from Karim. I can't imagine what this journey would have been without you."

Youssef chuckled, the lines of his face softening with pride. "You needed a safe path, and it was my honor to provide it. I knew from the first day that you two weren't ordinary travelers. You came with purpose, with respect, and the land responded to you."

He looked around, nodding to Rafiq, Amina, and the others, and then added, "Jordan will always be your second home. You have family here."

Simon reached out, shaking Youssef's hand firmly. "We owe you so much, Youssef. Not just for the rides and connections, but for every way you've looked out for us."

Youssef pulled Simon into a brief hug, then turned to Ellie with a warm grin, adding, "Just promise you won't forget us."

"Never," Ellie replied, feeling a tear slip down her cheek. "And you won't be rid of us that easily. We'll be back—count on it."

Nadia's smile grew as she spoke up, her tone filled with anticipation. "Oh, I have no doubt. Besides, I expect you to join us in Petra soon. We have a whole new dig under the Treasury awaiting us. The Ministry can hardly wait for the insights we'll uncover there."

Ellie and Simon exchanged a glance, excitement lighting up their faces as they thought of Petra and the discoveries it held. "A whole new chapter," Ellie said, grinning. "After a bit of family time back home, we'll be ready for the next adventure."

Youssef raised an eyebrow, smiling at them both. "Jordan will always have a place for you. And Petra has been waiting for travelers like you for centuries. Just don't keep her waiting too long."

With a final round of handshakes, hugs, and grateful smiles, Amina and Rafiq joined the others, watching as Ellie and Simon prepared to leave. Their faces reflected the deep connections that had been formed, connections that would endure well beyond this journey.

Simon glanced at his watch, his face reluctantly acknowledging the ticking clock. "I suppose it's time," he said, his voice tinged with sadness. They shared a long look, both recognizing the weight of the farewell.

Ellie took one last look at her friends, taking in their familiar faces, each one etched with memories of shared discoveries, laughter, and resilience. These were the people who had walked with her through one of the most profound journeys of her life, and it was difficult to leave them behind.

As Ellie and Simon entered the terminal, she felt Simon's arm slip around her shoulders, giving her a comforting squeeze. "They've become part of our story," he murmured, his voice thick with emotion. "It's hard to say goodbye."

Ellie leaned into him, finding comfort in his familiar warmth. "It's not really goodbye," she replied. "They'll always be with us, just as much as we'll always be with them. We've built something here—a connection that spans time and place. And we'll carry it with us."

Simon gave her a small smile, one that reflected his agreement. "Yes. And who knows? Maybe we'll all meet again sooner than we think."

As they boarded their flight, Ellie looked out the window, watching as the city of Amman stretched out beneath them. The landscape of Jordan lay in soft, warm tones, its desert expanses, ancient ruins, and vibrant cities forever imprinted on her heart.

She whispered a quiet farewell to the place that had transformed her life and renewed her sense of purpose. She knew that this journey was far from over—that the friends she was leaving behind, the stories she had uncovered, and the lessons she had learned would continue to guide her.

As the plane lifted off, she and Simon shared a look filled with anticipation and quiet resolve. They were returning home, but they were carrying with them a treasure more precious than any artifact: the bond of friendship, the wisdom of history, and the promise of future discoveries yet to come.

29

A FAMILY REUNITED

The familiar scent of home greeted Ellie and Simon as they stepped through the front door, the early evening light casting a warm glow across their living room. They had barely set down their bags when excited voices and footsteps echoed through the hallway as their children rushed toward them.

"Mom! Dad!" Benjamin called, reaching them first and pulling them into a tight embrace. Behind him, Oliver, Isabel, Sophie, and Nathan closed in, each of them smiling with relief and excitement.

"It feels like you've been gone forever!" Sophie exclaimed, her eyes bright as she hugged Ellie, holding on as though she never wanted to let go. "We were all following your journey. First the call about the dig, then the texts and FaceTimes from Jordan—my goodness, we were on the edge of our seats!"

Ellie and Simon took in the sight of their children's faces, marveling at how much they missed each of them. Their hearts swelled with gratitude as they shared hugs, laughter, and whispered words of love, feeling the reality of being home sink in.

Then, a small voice piped up from behind Sophie. "Nana? Grandpa?" Ellie's heart melted as she looked down and saw her grandson, Jacob, standing there, looking up at her with wide, curious eyes. He was three years old, his face a perfect mix of Sophie and Marco, with dark curls and big, expressive eyes.

"Jacob!" Ellie exclaimed, bending down and holding her arms open. Without hesitation, Jacob toddled forward, his little hands reaching for her. She pulled him close, feeling his warmth and hearing his small giggle as she peppered his cheeks with kisses. "I missed you so much, sweetheart!"

Simon joined her, ruffling Jacob's hair with a gentle hand. "My goodness, you've grown!" he said, his voice filled with wonder. "You're taller than me now!"

Jacob giggled, shaking his head, and gave Simon a big hug. "Nana and Grandpa, you came back!" he said proudly, looking up at both of them. "Mommy said you were on a big adventure."

Ellie chuckled, exchanging a look with Simon. "We sure were," she said with a smile. "And we have so many stories to tell you."

The family moved into the living room, where Isabel had set out a spread of tea, coffee, and some of Ellie's favorite snacks. They settled onto the couches, eager to catch up, and the room buzzed with warmth and anticipation.

"So," Nathan began, a glint of excitement in his eyes, "are you going to tell us everything, or are you keeping secrets from us?"

Simon laughed, glancing at Ellie. "Oh, I don't think we could keep any secrets even if we tried. The stories are too incredible to keep to ourselves."

Ellie leaned forward, her gaze moving around the circle of her children's faces. "As you all know, we were invited to Jordan by Dr. Nadia al-Masri, a brilliant archaeologist I'd met years ago. When we got that email invitation to join her, I felt like it was a chance we just couldn't pass up. The possibility of discovering a hidden temple in the desert? I mean, how could we say no?"

Oliver nodded, his expression serious. "We remember the group FaceTime that night—how excited you both were. But honestly, after that, we were worried, especially Nathan. You could see it all over his face during our calls."

Nathan nodded, looking at them both with a mixture of relief and awe. "You're right—I did worry. I mean, it sounded dangerous, and I know you two are adventurers, but... I had this gut feeling that you were walking into something big. Remember that FaceTime we had after I saw those reports of looting near Amman? I wanted to jump on a plane myself to keep you safe."

Ellie smiled at her youngest, feeling touched by his protectiveness. "I remember, Nathan. It meant so much that you cared that deeply. But we knew we had to face whatever came, especially when we realized just how precious the artifacts were to Jordan's heritage."

Simon nodded in agreement. "We were committed. And the dig site itself was breathtaking. Imagine ancient carvings emerging from the sands, fragments of symbols that hadn't seen daylight in centuries. We explored caves and chambers, even found a silver disc—like a treasure of old. I remember thinking, 'This is it, we're part of something timeless.'"

Sophie sighed, her voice filled with wonder. "It sounds magical. But I can't believe you also had to deal with someone like Karim. I mean, he actually tried to sabotage your work?"

Ellie's expression grew solemn. "Yes, Karim was after those artifacts for the black market. He threatened us, tried to scare us out, even orchestrated a break-in. He would have done anything to get those artifacts, but we had the support of people like Youssef, who helped protect us, and Rafiq, who offered us safe shelter. And of course, the Ministry's security team was invaluable. They helped us bring Karim down in the end."

"That's amazing," Benjamin said, shaking his head. "The lengths you went to, the risks you took... You didn't have to go that far, but you did."

Ellie smiled at him, reaching over to squeeze his hand. "But that's exactly why we had to go that far, Ben. These artifacts belonged to Jordan's people. It wasn't just about preserving history; it was about protecting a legacy."

Jacob, now sleepily curled in Ellie's lap, looked up at her with a yawn. "Nana, did you find treasure?"

Ellie chuckled and leaned in close to him. "Well, we didn't find treasure like in a pirate story, but we did find some shiny things. We found that silver disc, Jacob, with beautiful carvings on it. It was like a special treasure to the people who made it."

Jacob's eyes grew wide, and he whispered, "Wow."

As they continued sharing stories, the Whitcombe children updated their parents on their own lives. Isabel, ever the traveler, had just returned from a project in Spain, where she'd been studying sustainable design practices in ancient architecture.

"I kept thinking of you two while I was there," Isabel admitted, grinning. "You both inspire me to dig deeper, to look beyond what's on the surface."

Oliver shared that he'd been promoted at work, and Sophie spoke about new milestones with Jacob—his first drawing, his latest words, and his newfound obsession with dinosaurs. Benjamin and Nathan had both embarked on new projects, with Nathan revealing more about his small business venture, which he had only hinted at during his FaceTime call.

"Mom, Dad, when I called you back in Jordan, I didn't say much because things weren't finalized, but I've launched my own sustainable clothing line," Nathan explained, beaming with pride. "It's been a dream of mine, and I can't tell you how much watching you two pursue your passions inspired me to take the leap."

Ellie beamed, her heart swelling with pride as she looked around at each of her children. They had grown and flourished, each one following their dreams with the same spirit of exploration that had guided her and Simon.

"Oh, and there's more," Simon added, a glint of excitement in his eyes. "After we wrapped up the dig, we had a little downtime, and Nadia encouraged us to explore some of Amman's historic sites. We visited the Temple of Hercules—can you believe it? We'd read about it our whole lives, but nothing compares to standing there in person."

Ellie nodded, her eyes dreamy as she recalled the grandeur of the ancient ruins. "It was awe-inspiring, like stepping back in time. The views over the city, the towering columns, the sense of history—it's something I'll never forget."

Their children listened with fascination as Simon and Ellie described the sites of Amman, from the Citadel to the Roman Theater, each place steeped in stories and history. They spoke of how the ancient structures seemed to whisper of civilizations long gone and of the deep pride the Jordanian people had for their heritage.

"We have something else to share with you," Ellie began, her voice tinged with excitement. The children leaned in, sensing there was more to the story. Ellie and Simon exchanged a look, savoring the moment before continuing. "As a reward for the challenges we faced, the artifacts we recovered, and the heritage we helped protect, the Jordanian government has extended a truly special invitation," Ellie continued, her voice filled with pride. "They've invited us to participate in a new dig surrounding the Treasury in Petra."

The reaction from their children was immediate, filling the room with awe and admiration.

"You're going back to Jordan? To Petra?" Isabel asked, her eyes widening as a smile spread across her face.

"To the Treasury itself? The actual Treasury?" Oliver echoed, his tone filled with disbelief. "Mom, Dad... that's incredible. Petra is one of the most iconic places in the world!"

Ellie and Simon both laughed, caught up in their children's excitement. "Yes, we'll be right at the heart of it," Simon said, nodding. "This is one of the most significant archaeological sites in the region, and the invitation alone feels like the opportunity of a lifetime."

Nathan shook his head, his face breaking into a proud grin. "Of course they invited you! You practically fought off treasure hunters and criminals. It makes sense that they'd want you to protect and study a place like Petra. I can't think of anyone more deserving."

Sophie's voice softened, her expression full of admiration. "I can't believe it. Mom, Dad, you're going to be a part of history—at Petra, of all places! You'll uncover mysteries that have been hidden for centuries. We're so proud of you."

Ellie's heart swelled as she looked at her children's glowing faces. "Thank you. And yes, it's overwhelming to think about. But before we even think about stepping foot back in Jordan, we wanted to be home with all of you," she added, smiling. "It's family time first, adventure time later."

Jacob, who had been listening intently, piped up, his young voice filled with wonder. "Will there be more treasure?"

Ellie knelt beside him, gently stroking his curls. "Well, sweetheart, we don't know for sure. But Petra itself is like a treasure chest of secrets from the past. And while we might not find gold or jewels, we'll definitely bring back stories, just for you."

He beamed, nodding earnestly. "Bring me stories, Nana."

They talked well into the night, recounting tales of their stay at Amina's cozy home. "Amina was more than just a host," Ellie began, a warm smile crossing her face. "From the moment we arrived, she treated us like family. Her kindness wrapped around us like a blanket after those long days in the desert. Every evening, she'd insist on making us tea and bringing out these delicate sweets she'd baked herself. She'd sit with us in the courtyard, listening to our stories and sharing bits of her own life."

"Amina had this way of making every little thing feel special," Simon added. "She taught us about the local herbs she'd grown in her courtyard, each with its own meaning or history. And she even gave us small charms to carry into the desert. She called them her 'desert blessings.' It was her way of protecting us when she couldn't be there."

Ellie nodded, her expression thoughtful. "She'd tell us stories of her grandparents, who used to take her out into the desert when she was young. She had this incredible reverence for the land, like it was something sacred. And by the end of our stay, we felt it, too. We were living in her world—an ancient world—if only for a little while."

The children listened, captivated by the tales of Amina's generosity and warmth, and were visibly moved by the sense of belonging Ellie and Simon had found halfway across the world.

"And then there was Rafiq," Ellie continued. "We met him through Youssef, and I don't think we realized at first just how deeply he cared for us. But when things got dangerous, he didn't hesitate to protect us. He'd watch over us, even when we were out of his sight."

Sophie leaned forward, intrigued. "How did he help you?"

"During one of our worst moments, when Karim and his men were getting closer, Rafiq offered us a safe place to stay. It was as if he'd been waiting for the opportunity to help," Simon said. "And he didn't just protect us; he took on the responsibility of connecting us with people who could shield us further."

"He introduced us to Youssef," Ellie added, smiling at the memory of their loyal driver. "Youssef was just supposed to be our driver, but he became so much more. He had this quiet strength, like he was always thinking ahead, always prepared for anything. And when we needed it most, he showed up with the local authorities, tipping the scales in our favor when Karim thought he had us trapped."

"I'll never forget the way Youssef maneuvered through those narrow canyon roads," Simon said, shaking his head in admiration. "We were being chased, and he handled that vehicle like a pro. I swear he knew every twist and turn of the desert. We'd look at each other and just know that, in his hands, we were safe."

The children exchanged looks, clearly impressed by the courage of Youssef and Rafiq. "It sounds like you found true allies," Oliver said, nodding thoughtfully. "People who would do anything for you."

Ellie smiled. "Yes, allies and friends. They understood the risks we were facing. To them, it wasn't just about preserving history—it was about protecting something sacred."

They also recalled the support they'd received from their mentors at the university, Dr. Khalid Abbas and Professor Malik. "Dr. Abbas was one of the most knowledgeable historians I've ever met," Ellie said. "He'd stay late at the university with us, going over scrolls, manuscripts, and inscriptions with meticulous care."

"He had this incredible library," Simon added, his eyes lighting up at the memory. "Ancient texts, diagrams, rare books—you name it. He'd pull out an obscure manuscript or some crumbling document, and his eyes would light up as he'd explain its significance. He'd treat each discovery as if it were his own, investing hours to help us decode even the smallest symbols."

Ellie nodded, remembering Dr. Abbas's dedication. "Every time we'd make progress, he'd look at us with this intense pride, as though we were part of a shared mission. He'd say that the ancients left these stories behind for those willing to uncover them, and we were honored to be part of that.'"

"Then there was Professor Malik," Simon said, his voice thoughtful. "He had this air of mystery, like he knew things that went far beyond history books. Malik taught us to see beyond the artifacts. He'd walk with us through the ancient streets of Amman, describing the Nabatean traditions, their gods, their rituals. He once told us that everything we were looking for was right in front of us—we just had to look closely."

Ellie smiled. "Malik used to say we were 'walking in the footsteps of the ancients,' and he really meant it. He'd make us feel that every symbol, every carving had a purpose. It wasn't just history—it was a way of life."

"He'd tell stories about Nabatean traders, traveling through deserts to meet people from every corner of the ancient world," Simon continued. "To him, the past wasn't a distant thing—it was right there, part of our everyday work."

"Dr. Abbas and Professor Malik weren't just mentors; they became friends," Ellie said, her voice filled with warmth. "They gave us more than knowledge—they gave us their faith, their trust. I think, in some way, we became guardians of their legacy, too."

The children were captivated, absorbing the stories of Ellie and Simon's connection with their mentors and allies. Isabel's eyes shone as she leaned forward. "It sounds like this wasn't just about uncovering artifacts. It was about connecting with people, with their stories, and becoming part of something bigger."

Ellie nodded, her heart swelling with pride. "That's exactly what it was, Isabel. We may have been digging for ancient relics, but we found friends, mentors, and a sense of belonging that we didn't expect."

The evening wore on with laughter, more stories, and shared memories. Jacob drifted off to sleep in Ellie's arms, and one by one, the children excused themselves, heading to their rooms, leaving Ellie and Simon alone in the living room.

Simon looked at Ellie, his gaze tender. "You know," he began softly, "I didn't think it was possible, but I think I fell in love with you all over again on this trip."

Ellie's heart warmed as she leaned into him, resting her head on his shoulder. "Same here," she replied, her voice barely a whisper. "Seeing you out there, facing everything together, sharing this passion... it reminded me why I chose you all those years ago."

Simon wrapped an arm around her, pulling her close. "I couldn't have asked for a better partner, Ellie. You're my anchor and my compass, and every time I see you stepping into something new, it makes me want to do the same."

They sat together in silence, listening to the soft hum of the house, feeling their love deepen. They knew Jordan had changed them, adding a new layer of understanding and appreciation for each other.

Ellie placed a hand over his heart. "I never want to stop exploring with you, Simon. Wherever the world takes us, I want to be by your side."

Simon kissed her deeply, his voice full of emotion. "And I, by yours. No matter where we go, as long as we're together, I'm home."

The two of them sat together, wrapped in love and the certainty of new adventures yet to come. They had shared a journey that was both outward and inward, each step bringing them closer not only to history but to each other.

THE NEXT CHAPTER

The golden light of late afternoon poured through the windows, filling the Whitcombes' home with a soft, peaceful glow. Ellie sipped her tea, savoring the quiet hum of the house after the bustling days of family reunions and long conversations with their children. Life had settled into a familiar rhythm, yet both she and Simon could feel a subtle current of restlessness—an itch that began each time they'd glance at the artifacts and sketches they'd brought home from Jordan.

Simon was by her side, thumbing through his notebook, where he'd jotted down theories, sketches, and engineering possibilities he had observed in the ancient architecture during their time in the desert. His doctorate in technical engineering had never felt more relevant, and as he turned each page, his eyes lit up with a spark that Ellie recognized well.

"What's on your mind?" she asked, leaning over to catch a glimpse of his notes.

He chuckled, tapping a sketch he'd made of the ancient mechanisms they'd found hidden beneath one of the Jordanian ruins. "Do you remember how, during that dig, we found remnants of what looked like an ancient water distribution system? I can't shake the feeling that they used a more advanced system than we thought possible. It's like they were hiding technological secrets in plain sight."

Ellie's eyes sparkled with curiosity. "I remember. You were almost as excited about those findings as I was about the artifacts." She smiled, nudging him playfully. "I think that's when I realized that you'd caught the archaeology bug as much as I had."

Simon grinned, a gleam of determination in his eyes. "I wouldn't say I caught the bug. But after Jordan, I understand now that there's so much more to uncover, and so much of it has been hidden right under our feet for centuries. I'm fascinated by how ancient civilizations engineered their world, sometimes even outpacing what we assume to be modern ingenuity. It's... humbling."

Ellie leaned back, feeling a familiar surge of excitement wash over her. "You know, there's something timeless in that, isn't there? The way we're connected to these ancient builders, these storytellers who left pieces of their world behind."

Simon nodded, his gaze thoughtful. "Absolutely. I can see now why you've been so passionate about this work. The past isn't just a series of relics; it's a conversation that keeps going, across generations."

They sat in comfortable silence, both contemplating the journey they'd taken and the whispers of adventure that were stirring again. A part of Ellie was already wondering what it might be like to return to Petra for the next dig. But she knew that Petra was just one chapter in a larger story, one that could take them anywhere.

Suddenly, a message notification broke their reverie. Ellie picked up her phone and saw a familiar name: Dr. Olivia Marshall, an old friend and fellow archaeologist who was overseeing a dig in the highlands of Peru. Ellie's eyes widened as she read the message.

"Simon, you're not going to believe this." She handed him the phone, and he read the message aloud:

"Ellie, we've uncovered something remarkable at the site. It looks like a network of tunnels leading to a chamber with strange markings—patterns that seem to correspond to water flow, but nothing like we've seen before. We could really use someone with engineering expertise. Any chance you and Simon are ready for another adventure?"

Simon's brows lifted in intrigue, and he looked at Ellie, the corners of his mouth turning up in a smile. "So, what do you say? Ready to see the world from a different angle?"

Ellie laughed, already feeling the thrill of possibility. "Are you kidding? Peru? How could we say no?"

The thought of exploring new terrain—the highlands, with their rich history and vibrant culture—made Ellie's heart race. Peru held treasures from ancient civilizations that were still being uncovered, and it was clear that Dr. Marshall had stumbled upon something extraordinary.

Simon leaned back, his face a mixture of excitement and thoughtfulness. "I've always wanted to see those ancient Inca aqueducts up close. Their irrigation systems were ahead of their time, and I'd love to figure out how they managed to build a system that lasted centuries."

Ellie placed her hand on his, feeling the steady warmth of his touch. "It's perfect, isn't it? You'll get to dive into the technical side, and I'll get to piece together the history, the symbols, the stories." She paused, a soft smile spreading across her face. "Looks like we're not quite finished exploring, are we?"

Simon chuckled, his eyes twinkling. "It seems that the past isn't ready to let us go just yet."

Over the next week, as they made preliminary plans for their trip to Peru, they settled back into the rhythms of home life. But every now and then, they'd catch each other's gaze, knowing that the world was calling to them again, whispering of ancient mysteries and hidden histories waiting to be discovered.

One evening, as they sat on the porch watching the stars, Ellie turned to Simon, her eyes reflecting the starlight. "Do you ever wonder what drives us to keep going? To keep searching for stories that are thousands of years old?"

Simon thought for a moment before answering. "I think it's because every discovery reminds us that we're not alone. Every carving, every structure, every tool—it's all proof that people were here, that they built things to last, hoping someone would find them someday."

Ellie smiled, feeling a profound sense of connection to the explorers, builders, and dreamers of the past. "It's like a hand reaching out through time, isn't it? Inviting us to understand, to remember."

Simon wrapped an arm around her, pulling her close. "And here we are, answering that call. I think that's what I love most about this journey, Ellie. Not just the adventure, but knowing that, together, we're part of something far greater than ourselves."

They sat in silence for a long moment, savoring the peace of the evening and the unspoken promise of more discoveries yet to come. The highlands of Peru awaited, and beyond that, perhaps other places, other voices from the past calling out to be heard.

As they stood and walked back into the house, Ellie felt a wave of gratitude wash over her. She was home, and yet, with Simon by her side, every step felt like the beginning of a new adventure. It didn't matter where they went or what challenges lay ahead; they were bound by a shared love for the past, a passion for discovery, and the thrill of unraveling mysteries that connected them to all who had come before.

"Here's to the next chapter," she whispered, glancing over at Simon as they prepared to turn in for the night.

Simon met her gaze, his face lit with the same eagerness she felt. "To the next chapter," he replied, his voice soft but resolute.

As they turned out the lights, they knew that, wherever the world led them, they'd continue to walk the path of discovery together—forever students of the past, explorers at heart, with endless horizons stretching before them.

EPILOGUE: SECRETS
BENEATH THE TREASURY

The afternoon sun cast a warm, amber glow across Petra's rose-red sandstone, illuminating the intricate carvings on the Treasury's façade. Ellie and Simon stood shoulder to shoulder, gazing at the iconic structure with a mixture of reverence and excitement. While the world had come to recognize the Treasury from scenes in *Indiana Jones and the Last Crusade*, for the Whitcombes, it symbolized more than a cinematic marvel; it was a gateway to understanding one of history's most fascinating civilizations.

Petra had been a hidden treasure of its own for centuries, lost to the world until 1812, when Swiss explorer Johann Ludwig Burckhardt, disguised as an Arab traveler, stumbled upon it. Burckhardt's rediscovery pulled Petra from obscurity and introduced the world to the lost city of the Nabataeans, a civilization that flourished over two millennia ago. Known for their architectural ingenuity, the Nabataeans had carved elaborate facades, tombs, and temples directly into the sandstone cliffs of southern Jordan.

As Ellie and Simon walked through the winding, narrow gorge called the Siq—a natural stone pathway leading up to the Treasury—they marveled at the sheer scale of Petra.

The Treasury, or *Al-Khazneh*, was just one structure in a sprawling complex of tombs, temples, and amphitheaters that had once formed the heart of a bustling metropolis. For centuries, Petra had served as a vital trading hub, linking the Arabian Peninsula with the Mediterranean through the Incense Route. Spices, textiles, ivory, and silk flowed through Petra's markets, making it a melting pot of cultures, religions, and ideas.

Today, as the dig team gathered beneath the Treasury, the excitement was palpable. Dr. Nadia al-Masri, Amir, Layla, and the team they had come to think of as family were bustling around the base of the structure, setting up equipment and organizing artifacts. Ellie and Simon had barely unpacked their bags from their return to the U.S. when Nadia had called, inviting them to join a groundbreaking excavation beneath the Treasury.

"Welcome to Petra," Nadia said, her voice filled with pride as she embraced Ellie. "This is more than just an excavation—it's a chance to reveal the secrets that have been buried here for centuries."

The team was joined by two American archaeologists, Dr. Sarah Kendrick and Dr. Mark Reed, whose expertise in ancient architecture and preservation had brought them to Petra. Nadia introduced Ellie and Simon, and the archaeologists shared a respectful nod, knowing they were among colleagues with a shared love for discovery.

"We're glad to have you both here," Dr. Kendrick said warmly. "This site is extraordinary, and we need all the hands we can get. It's a monumental task—both figuratively and literally."

As they approached the entrance to the chamber beneath the Treasury, Simon's engineering mind went into overdrive. The Nabataeans had managed to carve this city directly into the rockface with remarkable precision, and their understanding of hydrology had enabled them to thrive in one of the most arid regions in the world. Petra was designed to be self-sustaining, with channels and cisterns that captured and directed rainwater throughout the city, creating a marvel of ancient urban planning.

Simon ran a hand along one of the carved channels, impressed by its design. "The Nabataeans weren't just builders," he said to Ellie. "They were engineers, architects, hydrologists. They created an oasis that supported a civilization for centuries."

Ellie nodded, her gaze shifting to the grand structure towering above them. "It's incredible to think that for centuries, people didn't even know Petra existed," she said. "But now, standing here, it feels alive—as if the Nabataeans never really left."

As Ellie and Simon took in the view of Petra's Treasury, the grandeur of the rose-red stone was just one part of the city's allure. Beneath the arid sands and towering cliffs lay traces of Petra's past as a thriving oasis—a place that was once lush and green, teeming with life. Ancient historians and scholars had long theorized that the Nabataean capital was far more verdant than the dry desert landscape it was now known for, an idea that archaeologists had increasingly supported with tangible evidence.

The Nabataeans were masters of water management, creating complex systems of aqueducts, cisterns, and channels to capture every precious drop of rainwater that fell. Some of these structures were still visible, carved directly into the rock walls, showcasing an ingenuity that allowed Petra to flourish. But these systems were more than mere utilities; they were the lifeblood of an agricultural society that supported groves of olive trees, grapevines, and fertile fields of crops—a stark contrast to the barren, dusty landscape that surrounds Petra today.

Studies of ancient pollen grains and seeds from Petra's soil hinted at an oasis once rich with vegetation. These remnants suggested that Petra was not only a bustling trading hub but also a center for agriculture, with fields terraced into the cliffs and gardens thriving within its valleys. Ellie found herself imagining how the lush landscape would have softened the rose-colored sandstone, casting Petra as an inviting jewel amidst the desert—a city that could sustain itself and welcome travelers from every corner of the ancient world.

"Imagine what it must have been like," Ellie murmured, "to walk into this hidden city and find it filled with greenery, fruit-bearing trees, and flowing water."

Simon nodded, running his fingers along the edge of one of the water channels carved into the Treasury's base. "The Nabataeans built systems that could sustain life here for centuries, capturing rainwater and storing it in hidden cisterns and reservoirs. They must have seen this city as something sacred—part temple, part sanctuary."

Their colleague, Dr. Kendrick, joined them, pointing to the channels that extended beyond the Treasury, weaving through the complex in an intricate network. "These aqueducts were part of an advanced irrigation system. The Nabataeans may have lived in a desert, but their knowledge of water management allowed them to create a city that could withstand even the driest years."

Ellie and Simon exchanged a glance, each sensing the marvel of Petra's transformation over the centuries. Once an oasis on the Incense Route, the city had evolved from a lush trading hub into a symbol of resilience and mystery, guarded by time and the encroaching desert sands. Yet here they stood, uncovering layer by layer, rediscovering Petra not only as a wonder of the ancient world but as a testament to the ingenuity and tenacity of the people who had once thrived within its walls.

Just then, Amir called them over to the main excavation area, where ground-penetrating radar had recently revealed an underground chamber. The chamber had turned out to be a hidden tomb containing twelve well-preserved skeletons, as well as various ceremonial artifacts that had lain untouched for nearly two millennia.

"We've found a burial site with relics that seem to suggest a high-ranking family," Dr. Kendrick explained as she guided Ellie and Simon through the entrance to the chamber. "The Nabataeans were a fascinating civilization, but they left very few written records. Everything we know about them comes from artifacts and architecture."

Inside the chamber, the air was cool and still. Ellie's eyes adjusted to the dim light, and she took in the stone walls covered with intricate carvings. These were not just decorative; each symbol told a story. There were scenes depicting the Nabataeans' gods and goddesses, symbols of fertility, prosperity, and protection. In the center of the room stood a stone slab, upon which lay a beautifully carved bronze vessel.

Ellie picked up the vessel carefully, marveling at the craftsmanship. The engravings along the edge depicted scenes of ritual offerings and ceremonial gatherings. "This was more than just a burial site," she said softly. "It was a place of reverence—a space where the Nabataeans believed they could connect with their gods."

Dr. Reed joined them, studying the carvings closely. "What's fascinating is that the Nabataeans incorporated so many influences. You can see traces of Greco-Roman, Egyptian, and Mesopotamian elements here. Petra was truly a crossroads of ancient civilizations."

As the team meticulously cataloged each artifact, Simon became engrossed in the engineering marvel of Petra's design. He examined a series of small channels carved into the stone floor, which, according to Amir, had likely been used to redirect water as part of a purification ritual. Simon traced the channels with his fingers, feeling the precision of each line.

"These channels are more than just functional," he said to Amir. "They're symbolic. Water was life to the Nabataeans, and they understood its power. They created a system that not only supported their city but reflected their spiritual beliefs."

Amir nodded, a hint of awe in his voice. "The Nabataeans knew the desert better than anyone. They mastered it. They thrived where others would have perished."

Layla, who had been carefully studying a pottery shard nearby, suddenly spoke up. "Ellie, look at this," she said, holding up a fragment inscribed with a faint Nabataean blessing. "Dr. Abbas thinks it's meant to protect the spirits of those who are buried here."

Ellie examined the shard, feeling the reverence with which it had been crafted. The words, barely discernible, seemed to echo the Nabataeans' faith, their connection to a world beyond. "It's like they left a message for us," she murmured. "A reminder that their lives, their beliefs, are still with us."

Outside the chamber, the sounds of the dig continued as workers carefully unearthed more artifacts, each one adding to the story of Petra. As the sun began to set, casting a golden glow over the Treasury, the team gathered for a moment of quiet reflection. Professor Malik raised a small, chipped cup he'd found in one of the tombs, filled it with water, and held it up in a silent toast to the Nabataeans and their enduring legacy.

"To the past," he said, his voice carrying a sense of solemn respect, "and to those who preserve it."

Ellie, Simon, and the others lifted their own cups, feeling a sense of unity with those who had come before them. Petra had opened itself to them, revealing secrets that had been guarded for centuries. It was an honor, a responsibility, and a connection to history that transcended time.

As the stars appeared over the Treasury, twinkling against the rose-colored cliffs, Nadia turned to Ellie, a satisfied smile on her face. "This isn't just an excavation, Ellie," she said. "This is a legacy. A story we are all part of."

Ellie looked around at the faces of her colleagues—Amir, Layla, Dr. Kendrick, Dr. Reed, Malik, and Abbas—and felt a profound sense of belonging. "I'm so grateful to be a part of this journey," she said, her voice filled with gratitude.

After a final glance at the Treasury, they began the walk back to camp, each step echoing the footsteps of those who had walked this path thousands of years before. As Ellie and Simon walked side by side, they knew this was not the end of their journey. The ancient city of Petra had more stories to tell, and they would be there to listen.

Milton Keynes UK
Ingram Content Group UK Ltd.
UKHW040158211124
451476UK00010B/94

9 781991 296061